HARLEQUIN®
Presents~

A warm welcome to all our readers; it's cold outside, but the books Harlequin Presents has got for you in January will leave you positively glowing!

Raise your temperature with two right royal reads! *The Sheikh's Innocent Bride,* by top author Lynne Graham, whisks you away to the blazing dunes of the desert in a classic tale of a proud sheikh's desire for the young woman employed to clean his castle. Meanwhile, Robyn Donald is back with another compelling Bagaton story in *The Royal Baby Bargain,* the latest installment in her immensely popular New Zealand-based BY ROYAL COMMAND miniseries.

Want the thermostat turned up? Then why not travel with us to the glorious Greek islands, where *Bought by the Greek Tycoon,* by favorite author Jacqueline Baird, promises searing emotional scenes and nights of blistering passion, and Susan Stephens's *Virgin for Sale*—the first title in our steamy new miniseries UNCUT—sees an uptight businesswoman learning what it is to feel pleasure in the hands of a *real* man!

For Cathy Williams fans, there's a new winter warmer: in *At the Italian's Command,* the heart of a notoriously cool, workaholic tycoon is finally melted by a frumpy but feisty journalist. And try turning the pages of rising star Melanie Milburne's latest release—*Back in her Husband's Bed,* about a marriage rekindled in sunny Sydney, Australia, is *almost* too hot to handle!

For a full list of titles and book numbers, see inside the front cover (opposite)—and enjoy!

Surrender To The Sheikh

He's proud, passionate, primal—
dare she surrender to the sheikh?

Feel warm winds blowing through your hair
and the hot desert sun on your skin as you are
transported to exotic lands....As the temperature
rises, let yourself be seduced by our sexy,
irresistible sheikhs.

If you love our men of the desert,
look for more stories in this enthralling
miniseries coming soon in April:
Traded to the Sheikh
by Emma Darcy
#2530
Available only from Harlequin Presents®.

Lynne Graham

THE SHEIKH'S INNOCENT BRIDE

Surrender To
The Sheikh

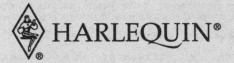

HARLEQUIN®

TORONTO • NEW YORK • LONDON
AMSTERDAM • PARIS • SYDNEY • HAMBURG
STOCKHOLM • ATHENS • TOKYO • MILAN • MADRID
PRAGUE • WARSAW • BUDAPEST • AUCKLAND

ISBN 0-373-12511-9

THE SHEIKH'S INNOCENT BRIDE

First North American Publication 2006.

Copyright © 2005 by Lynne Graham.

This edition published by arrangement with Harlequin Books S.A.

® and TM are trademarks of the publisher. Trademarks indicated with ® are registered in the United States Patent and Trademark Office, the Canadian Trade Marks Office and in other countries.

www.eHarlequin.com

Printed in U.S.A.

All about the author...
Lynne Graham

Born of Irish/Scottish parentage, Lynne Graham has lived in Northern Ireland all her life. She has one brother. She grew up in a seaside village and now lives in a country house surrounded by a woodland garden, which is wonderfully private.

Lynne first met her husband when she was fourteen. They married after she completed her degree at Edinburgh University. Lynne wrote her first book at fifteen and it was rejected everywhere. She started writing again when she was at home with her first child. It took several attempts before she sold her first book and the delight of seeing that first book for sale in the local store has never been forgotten.

Lynne always wanted a large family and has five children. Her eldest, and her only natural child, is in her twenties and a university graduate. Her other children, who are every bit as dear to her heart, are adopted: two from Sri Lanka and two from Guatemala. In Lynne's home, there is a rich and diverse cultural mix, which adds a whole extra dimension of interest and discovery to family life.

The family has two pets. Thomas is a very large and affectionate black cat, and Daisy is an adorable but not very bright white West Highland terrier, who loves being chased by the cat. At night, dog and cat sleep together in front of the kitchen stove.

Lynne loves gardening, cooking, collecting everything from old toys to rock specimens and is crazy about every aspect of Christmas.

CHAPTER ONE

HIS SERENE HIGHNESS, Prince Shahir bin Harith al-Assad, reached his vast estate in the Scottish Highlands shortly before eight in the morning.

As usual, every possible arrangement had been put in place to smooth his arrival with the seamless luxury that had been his right since birth. A limousine with blacked-out windows had collected him from the private airfield where his Lear jet had landed. At no stage had anyone sought to breach his reserve with unwelcome dialogue, for he valued his privacy beyond all other things and his staff worked hard at keeping the rest of the world at bay. Offered a seat in the limo, his estate manager, Fraser Douglas, had answered several questions and then embraced a self-effacing silence.

The only road to Strathcraig Castle stretched for more than fifteen miles, through tawny moorlands surrounded by spectacular purple-blue mountains. The lonely silence of the majestic landscape and the wide blue sky that filled the horizon reminded Shahir of the desert that he loved with an even greater passion. After the frenetic bustle and buzz of the business world, the wild, natural emptiness refreshed his eyes.

As the limo began its descent into the remote forested glen of Strathcraig the passage of a flock of sheep forced the powerful vehicle to a halt. A white-haired woman with a bicycle was also waiting by the side of the road. Only when she turned her head did Shahir appreciate that the woman had barely left her teenage years behind: her hair was not white, it was a very pale platinum-blonde, drawn back from her delicate features in smooth wings. Slender and graceful, she had wide, intelligent eyes and a sensitive, full pink mouth. Even her drab clothing could not conceal the fact that she was as proud and pure in her beauty as an angel he had once seen in an illuminated manuscript. There was, however, nothing reverent about the instant charge of lust that she ignited in Shahir. He was startled by the unfamiliar intensity of his desire, for it had been a long time since a woman had excited his interest to that extent

'Who is that?' he asked the estate manager seated opposite him.

'Kirsten Ross, Your Highness,' the square-faced older man advanced, and when the silence lay gathering dust, in a way that implied he had answered too briefly, he hastened to offer more facts. 'I believe she's employed as a domestic at the castle.'

Shahir would not have dreamt of bedding an employee, and the news that she worked for him in so menial a capacity struck an even less welcome note, for he was a fastidious man. 'I haven't seen her before.'

'Kirsten Ross isn't the sort to draw attention to herself.'

Hard cynicism firmed Shahir's well-sculpted mouth. He was a connoisseur of beautiful women, and had yet to meet one unaware of her power. 'She must be accustomed to the attention her looks excite.'

'I shouldn't think she's ever been encouraged to pay much heed to a mirror,' Fraser Douglas responded with a wry grimace. 'Her father is a religious fanatic with a reputation for being very strict on the home front.'

Realising in some surprise that he was still staring at

the exquisite blonde, Shahir averted his attention with punctilious care from her. The car drove on.

The older man's censorious reference to the girl's father had surprised him, for where did religious devotion end and fanaticism begin? After all, to an outsider village life in Strathcraig appeared to revolve round the church and its activities. The local community followed a very different code of values from the more liberal ways of high society circles. Indeed, the tenants on the estate had a conservative outlook that struck visitors as distinctly grim and outdated, and was probably the result of the glen's isolation from the wider world.

Yet Shahir was more at home at Strathcraig than he was within a more *laissez-faire* culture. Dhemen, the Middle Eastern kingdom of his birth, was equally strait-laced. Right was right and wrong was wrong and community welfare always took precedence over the freedom of the individual. Within that clear framework few dared to stray, and those who did were punished by the opprobrium they attracted.

In much the same way Shahir accepted the limitations that fate had chosen to place on his own prospects of happiness. Any woman he took to his bed could only be a poor substitute for the one he really desired, he acknowledged wryly. He loved a woman who could never be his, and casual sexual affairs were his only outlet. But he was thirty-two years old, and that was not how he had planned to live his life.

Concerned relatives kept on lining up the names of promising bridal prospects, and the more broad-minded set up casual meetings with suitable females on his behalf. Perhaps, he reflected grimly, it was time for him to bite the bullet and choose one of those candidates. His darkly handsome features firmed. An Arabian woman would devote her energies 24/7 to the pursuit of being his wife. In return she would expect children, wealth, and the prestige of great position. Love wouldn't come into the equation and why should it? Marriage in his world had much more to do with the practicalities of status, family connections and, primarily, the provision of an heir. His father had been extremely sympathetic towards his son's desire to remain single for as long as possible but, as the next in line to the throne, Shahir was well aware that he could not stave off the inevitable for much longer.

It was fortunate that there was not an atom of romance in his soul, Shahir conceded with bleak satisfaction. His hot-blooded temperament and powerful sex-drive had always been kept in line by his strong principles and his discriminating tastes. He was a man who faced the truth, no matter how unpalatable it was. He was not a man who made foolish mistakes. Born into the very heart of a royal family, he knew what his duty entailed and he was proud of his heritage. His keen intelligence told him that accepting the need to acquire a wife would be a much more sensible option than eying up a gorgeous but totally unsuitable Western woman—particularly one who worked for him in so lowly a capacity…

'You're living in Cloud-cuckoo-land,' Jeanie Murray told Kirsten with blunt conviction as she sat on the worn wooden counter, smoking a cigarette in flagrant disregard of her rules of employment. 'Your father will never let you live away from home to go to college.'

Kirsten continued to wash a bone-thin Sevres china saucer with gentle and careful hands, her classic profile intent. 'I think that now that he's married to Mabel he might be prepared to consider it.'

'Aye, all that kneeling and praying didn't stop your dad from courting a new bride before your poor mum was cold in her grave. Folk say he likes his home comforts on tap.' Impervious to her companion's discomfiture, the plump, freckled redhead rolled her eyes and vented a laugh. 'But why should he agree to you moving out? You're bringing home a tidy pay packet. Don't tell me that that isn't welcome to Angus Ross—we all know how tight his hold is on his wallet!'

Kirsten tried not to wince at the news that her father's stinginess was a living legend locally. Jeanie's frankly uttered opinions and tactless remarks often caused friction with other members of staff. Kirsten, however, could forgive her much, for she valued the other woman's warm-hearted friendliness. 'Jeanie…'

'Don't go all goody-goody on me just because you think you should. You know it's true. I've heard a story or two about what your home life's like, and that's no picnic by all accounts—'

'But I don't discuss my family with anyone,' Kirsten slotted in swiftly.

Jeanie rolled her eyes with unblemished good humour. 'I bet you're still doing all the cooking and cleaning at home. Old sourpuss Mabel won't want you to move out either. Face up to it, Kirsten. You're twenty-two years old and the only way you're ever going to get a life of your own is by running away as fast as your legs can carry you from the pair of them!'

'We'll see.' Kirsten bent her head and said nothing more.

It would take a hefty sum of money to enable her to set up home elsewhere. Running away would be the coward's way out, and doing so without sufficient funds would be foolish, for it would land her straight into the poverty trap. She wanted to be able to rent somewhere decent and plan her future. She just had to be patient, she reminded herself sternly. She was only six weeks into her very first job, and with her father taking a large slice of her wages to cover her keep it would be a few months before her savings could cover any sort of a move.

She could wait until then; her job, humble as it was, still felt like a lifeline to her. She loved working in the medieval splendour of the historic castle. The magnificent surroundings were an endless source of fascination to her. Even riding her bike into work every morning gave her a freedom that had long been denied her. The chance to mix freely with other people was even more welcome. But she was equally conscious that she wanted more out of life than a post as a cleaner, and that she needed qualifications and training to aspire to anything more.

Yet the prospect of having to blatantly defy her father's rigid rules of conduct was challenging and frightening, for she had been taught from childhood to offer him unquestioning obedience. He was a cold, intimidating man, with a violent temper that she had once struggled to protect her late mother from. Her lovely face shadowed, for she was still grieving for that loss.

Isobel Ross had become ill when her daughter was thirteen years old, and her long, slow decline had been matched by her ever greater need for care. That responsibility had fallen on Kirsten's shoulders. Her father had not been prepared to assist with what he saw as 'women's work', and her older brother, Daniel, had been kept too busy doing farm work to be in any position to help. Once the brightest child in her class, Kirsten had begun to miss a great deal of school and her grades had slowly worsened.

Fed up with the restrictions imposed by their father's

increasingly obsessive absorption in religion, her brother had finally quarrelled with him and moved out. As soon as it was legally possible, Angus Ross had removed his daughter from school so that she could nurse her mother and take charge of his household.

For the following five years Kirsten had only left the farm to attend church and do the weekly shop. Her father disapproved of social occasions and had discouraged all visitors. Exactly a year after her mother's death her father had married Mabel. The other woman was sour and sharp-tongued. But Kirsten was grateful that Mabel's eagerness to see more money coming into the household had prompted her stepmother to persuade her husband to allow Kirsten to seek employment outside the home.

'We'll have to see if we can get you a proper thrill this week, while our gorgeous desert sheikh is in residence,' Jeanie remarked brightly.

A surprisingly mischievous smile curved Kirsten's lips. 'I've had my treat for the week: I saw the Prince's limousine, and very impressive it was too.'

'Never mind the limo. We'll hide you somewhere to get a glimpse of the man himself! I've only seen him a couple of times, and at a distance, but I'm telling you he'd make a sinner out of any saint.' Jeanie groaned, with a lascivious look in her eyes, as she disposed of her cigarette and put the ashtray back in its hiding place. 'He's a right sex god.'

'I'll be keeping well out of his way. I wouldn't want to lose my job.' Kirsten had been warned when she was hired that all domestic tasks at the castle were to be carried out with as much silence and invisibility as was humanly possible. It had been made equally clear to her that if her phenomenally rich and royal employer was to appear in the same corridor she was to hastily vacate it, so she didn't think there would be much chance of her bumping into him!

'If I had your face and body I'd be tripping over myself to accidentally fall in His Serene Highness's way!' Jeanie gave her a broad wink.' If he fancied you he could take you away from all this and set you up in a house somewhere. You'd be *made*, because he's minted! Think of the clothes you could have, and the jewels, and a real macho man in your bed into the bargain. You're really beautiful, Kirsten. If anyone could pull Prince Shahir, you could!'

Kirsten studied her in bewilderment, her colour rising. 'I'm not like that—'

'Well, you'd be much better off if you were,' the redhead told her roundly. 'At least I know how to have a bit of fun and I can enjoy a good laugh. If you don't watch out your father will turn you into a dried-up old spinster!'

Having finished washing the Sevres dinner service, Kirsten dried it piece by piece with great care. Even so, her thoughts were miles away. She felt so out of step with Jeanie. Kirsten had been brought up in a house where the only spoken reference to sex had related to what her father referred to as 'the sin of fornication'. The content of the newspapers and magazines she had glimpsed since starting work at the castle had initially shocked her, for the only written matter in her home consisted of the Bible and religious tracts, and it was many years since her father had got rid of the television. Yet she was guiltily aware that she was sorely tempted by the fashionable clothes and the exotic places that she had seen in those publications.

If only her father were a more reasonable man. If only he would allow her to go out and about and enjoy mixed company, like other women her age. After all, he must have dated her late mother to have married her—and surely that could not have been morally wrong?

Her father was growing terrifyingly unreasonable in his attitudes and his demands. After a dispute with the church elders, the older man would no longer attend church, and Kirsten and Mabel had been forced to stay home as well. Kirsten loved music. One of her few pleasures had been her radio, and he had broken that in a fit of rage when Mabel complained that her stepdaughter spent so much time listening to it that she was late making breakfast. Mabel had been shaken by her husband's reaction, though, Kirsten recalled heavily. It was small comfort for her to suspect that her stepmother was not wholly content with her hasty second marriage.

'Would you like it?' At lunchtime another member of staff extended the magazine she had been reading to Kirsten. 'It's OK...I'm finished with it.'

Her face suffused with self-conscious pink, Kirsten accepted the item with a muttered word of thanks. As she left the basement staffroom, she heard the woman say, 'It's a pity about her, isn't it? Angus Ross should be hung for treating her the way he does! She's scared of her own shadow!'

No, I'm *not*, Kirsten thought, frantically pedalling away her hurt pride and resentment as she headed home on her bike. She was not scared of her own shadow— but neither was she mad enough to go head to head with her father before she had the means to leave his home.

The beauty of the early summer day soon calmed her temper and raised her spirits. After all it was a Friday, and her favourite day of the week. On Fridays she finished work early, and the house would be empty whilst Mabel and her father did the weekly grocery shopping.

Afterwards they would visit Mabel's elderly mother, and remain with her for their evening meal. Kirsten decided to take her dog for a walk and read the magazine.

Half an hour later she walked through her father's fields, which led right up to the edge of the forest. She was dismayed to see that fresh tyre tracks had torn up the soft ground, leaving messy furrows of mud that would fill with water when the rain came. Her father had been outraged a few weeks earlier, when a pair of yobs on motorbikes had torn up a newly sown field. News of a second visit and further damage to the land would put Angus Ross into the kind of temper that made Kirsten suck in her breath in dismay.

Deciding that it would be wiser to let her father discover the damage for himself, she crossed the stile that marked the boundary of the farm and followed a little-used path up through the forest to the top of the hill. She kicked off her shoes, undid a couple of buttons at the neck of her blouse, and loosened her hair to relax in the sunshine. Her dog, Squeak, a small, short-legged animal of mixed ancestry, sank down in the middle of the grassy path, for the steep climb had exhausted him. His perky little ears did not prick up at the distant growl of an engine across the valley for as his age had advanced his hearing had steadily become more impaired.

Kirsten began to devour her magazine, and before very long was absorbed to the exclusion of all else in the delightful world of celebrities, fabulous fashion and wicked gossip.

One minute she was dreaming in the sunlight, the next she was jerking up from her reclining position with a stricken exclamation as a giant black motorbike burst with a roar over the hill and headed straight for Squeak. Kirsten made a violent lunge at the old dog to grab him out of the way. Mere feet from her, the bike skidded at fantastic and terrifying speed off the track, and the rider went flying up into the air. Horror stopped her breathing. But, in what seemed like virtually the same moment, he hit the ground and rolled with the spectacular, almost acrobatic ease of a jockey taking a fall.

Kirsten looked on wide-eyed as the rider, who was clearly uninjured, vaulted back upright again. Her shock was engulfed by a flood of unfamiliar anger.

'You're trespassing!' she heard herself yell at the impossibly tall black-leather-clad figure approaching her as she scrambled up.

Shahir was furious with her for sitting in the middle of a track, like a target waiting for a direct hit from on high. She was very fortunate not to have been killed. He could not credit that she was shouting at him—nobody ever shouted at him—but, perhaps fortunately for her, the alluring picture that she made clouded that issue. Her shimmering silvery blonde hair was loose round her narrow shoulders and fell almost to her waist in a stunning display of luxuriance. He encountered eyes that were not the Celtic blue he had expected, but the verdant green of emerald and moss. His attention was by then irretrievably locked to her, and he noticed that she was surprisingly tall for a woman. As tall as his Berber ancestors himself, he stood six feet five in his socks, but barefoot she was still tall enough to reach his chin.

'In fact, not only are you trespassing—'

'I am not a trespasser,' he countered, his dark, deep voice muffled by the black helmet which concealed his face from her.

'This is private ground, so you *are* trespassing.' As far as Kirsten was concerned his failure to offer an immediate apology merely added insult to injury, and her soft mouth compressed. 'Don't you realise how fast you were going?'

'I know exactly what my speed was,' Shahir confirmed.

He might behave like a yob, but he didn't speak quite as she had assumed he would. His accent was unmistakably English and upper class, his crystal-clear vowel sounds crisply pronounced in spite of the helmet. She told herself off for being so biased in her expectations. A tourist toff could be just as much of a hooligan as a yob out for a day biking through the hills. Her chin took on a stubborn tilt.

'Well, you frightened the life out of me and my dog!' she asserted, lowering her arms to let Squeak down , his solid little body having become too heavy for comfort.

Far from behaving like a traumatised animal, Squeak padded over to Shahir's booted feet, nuzzled them, wagged his tail in a lazily friendly fashion and then ambled off to curl up and sleep in the sunshine.

'At least he's not shouting at me as well.' Shahir said dryly.

'I wasn't shouting.' Her lilting accent took on a clipped edge of emphasis. His refusal to admit fault was testing even Kirsten's tolerant nature. 'You could have killed me…you could have killed yourself!'

Shahir flipped up his visor. Kirsten stilled. Her first thought was that he had the eyes of a hawk from the castle falconry: steady, unblinking, unnervingly keen. But his gaze was also a spectacular bronze-gold in colour, enhanced by lashes lush as sable and dark as ebony. Her heart jumped behind her breastbone and suddenly she was conscious of its measured beat. Indeed, it was as if her every sense had gone on to super-alert and time had slowed its passage.

'Don't exaggerate,' Shahir drawled.

'You were travelling at a crazy speed...' she framed breathlessly.

Shahir watched the sun transform her hair to a veil of shining silver that he longed to touch. He was so taken aback by the inappropriate desire that for the first time in his life he forgot what he was about to say. 'Was I?'

He pulled off his helmet and smoothed back his ruffled black hair with long brown fingers. Kirsten's mouth ran dry. He was so exceptionally handsome that she simply stared. He also had the most unforgettable face. His fantastic bone structure was composed of high, slashing cheekbones and sleek planes and hollows, divided by a strong, masculine nose and defined by level dark brows. His bronzed complexion and very black hair suggested an ancestry at variance with his beautifully enunciated English. Every aspect of him offered a source of immediate fascination to her. She felt dizzy, as if she had been spinning round and round like a child and had suddenly stopped to find her balance gone. A tiny twist of something she had never felt before pulled low in her pelvis.

'Were you what?' she mumbled, belatedly striving to recall the conversation.

The hint of a smile tilted the beautiful curve of his mouth. She was as enchanted by the movement of his sculpted lips as though a magic wand had been waved over her.

'I always travel at a crazy speed on the motorbike. But I'm a very safe rider.'

Kirsten made a frantic attempt to rescue her wits. 'But you couldn't even see where you were going,' she reminded him.

Shahir was not accustomed to a consistent reminder of his apparent oversight, and he fought back. 'Should I expect to find a woman and a dog parked in the centre of the track?'

'Perhaps not…but you *are* on private land—'

'I know—and I knew there were no livestock up here. This is *my* land.'

Kirsten giggled. 'No, it's not. I live just down the hill, and you can't fool me.'

'Can't I?' Shahir watched amusement light up her exquisite face and realised that she assumed he was teasing her. She genuinely had no idea of his identity.

But the sound of that unfamiliar light-hearted giggle emerging from her own lips had startled Kirsten. Her eyes veiled, and dropped from his in dismay. She was finally recalling the furrows ploughed on her father's ground at the foot of the hill, and she was dismayed that she had contrived to forget what she had seen.

'This isn't your first visit here, though, is it?' she said tautly. 'You and your motorcycle have already made a mess of the field below the forest!'

Incredulous at the sudden accusation, Shahir surveyed her with narrowed eyes that had the subtle gleam of rapier blades. 'Now you are talking nonsense. I respect the field boundaries. I am not a teenage vandal.'

Kirsten coloured, but persisted. 'Well, it seems to me that it's too much of a coincidence to be anyone else but you who was responsible. Someone has been in that field within the last few days, and there's been a lot of damage done.'

'It was not I. You should not make such an allegation without evidence to support it,' Shahir condemned, with a gravity that was very much at odds with the apparent casualness of his motorbike leathers. 'I find it offensive.'

His measured intonation made her pale. His dark gaze was uncompromisingly direct, and he spoke with a clear authority that unnerved her. Involuntarily, for she had lowered her scrutiny, she stole a glance at him. Her eyes glittered like jade in the pale oval of her face. 'I find it offensive that you haven't even said sorry for giving me the fright of my life.'

The silence lay like a charge of dynamite already lit.

An almost imperceptible touch of colour highlighted his superb cheekbones; Shahir had always cherished the belief that he was innately courteous. 'Naturally I offer you my apologies for scaring you.'

'Well, if it wasn't you who cut up my father's field,' Kirsten said doubtfully, 'I'm sorry I suggested it was.'

Shahir bent down with fluid grace and swept up the magazine lying abandoned on the ground and extended it to her. 'You were reading?'

'Yes...thanks.' Suddenly aware of his keen regard, Kirsten blushed to the roots of her hair and dragged her attention from him, wondering in a panic of embarrassment if he was staring at her only because she had been staring at him.

A sweet, savage hunger gripped Shahir as he studied her downbent head and luscious pink mouth. He let his attention roam to the pouting fullness of her small full breasts. His body hardened with an ardent masculine urgency that shook him.

Kirsten was conscious of the tense atmosphere, and of the inexplicable sense of excitement trying to pull at her senses. She did not understand its source, for it filled her with too much confusion. While one part of her wanted to run away, the rest of her wanted to prolong the meeting. She fumbled frantically for something to say. 'Is your motorbike going to be all right?'

'I believe so.' He had mastered his hunger with fierce self-discipline, and Shahir's drawl was as cool and discouraging as a shower of rain. He was annoyed by his own brief loss of control. Admittedly, she was very beautiful, but he was used to gorgeous women. Perhaps, he reasoned, there was something especially appealing about such natural loveliness and unmistakable modesty when he was usually accustomed to meeting with boldness.

'Have you far to go?' Kirsten muttered, scarcely crediting her own daring. But at that moment all she was aware of was that he was about to walk away and she didn't want him to.

'Only to the castle.' Shahir strode over to the fallen machine and hauled it up out of the flattened grass with strong hands. He could have told her who he was, but he saw no point in embarrassing her when it was unlikely that they would ever meet again. Someone else would soon tell her of the mistake she had made.

He was staying at Strathcraig Castle as a guest? Why hadn't that occurred to her before? It was, after all, the most obvious explanation for the presence of a well-spoken stranger in the glen. Dismay replaced the daze that she had been wrapped in and her skin chilled. She had offended him, hadn't she? Would he complain about her? Say she had been rude to him? Accusing him of vandalism had certainly not been the way to demonstrate a hospitable welcome to a visitor. What on earth had come over her? She shouldn't have said a single critical word to him. After all, if she was sacked she would never find another job locally, and her father would be outraged.

Shahir replaced his helmet and fired the engine of the powerful motorbike, looking back at her only for an instant before he took off back down the track again. With him travelled the image of glorious green eyes pinned to him with anxious intensity. He wondered what sort of a life she had, with the fanatical father his estate manager had mentioned. She looked scared and unhappy.

A split second later, without any warning whatsoever of the trick his cool and rational brain was about to play on him, Shahir was startled to find himself wondering how Kirsten Ross might adapt to being a mistress. *His* mistress. The instant the idea occurred to him he was exasperated by the vagaries of his own mind; that type of arrangement was certainly not his style. He was a generous lover, who offered commitment for the duration of an affair. But the affairs began and ended without touching his heart or even his temper. Sex was a pleasure to be savoured, but his libido did not control him and he sought nothing more lasting from the women who entertained him in bed.

In short, a mistress would be a radical new departure for him. She would have a semi-permanent role in his life, and would be dependent on him in a way that he had never allowed a woman to be. It was an insane idea for a male who enjoyed his freedom to the extent that he did, Shahir acknowledged with a brooding frown. What was more Kirsten Ross was an employee, and as such strictly out of bounds; Shahir was a man of honour. What the hell was the matter with him? One minute he was thinking of taking a wife, the next a mistress—and all in the space of twenty-four hours!

Having dug a hole in the soft ground below the trees and buried the magazine, Kirsten ran most of the way home, with Squeak gasping at her heels. Unlocking the back door, she sped through it, only to be brought up short by the dismaying sight of the thickset man lodged in stillness at the back of the sparsely furnished kitchen.

'I wasn't expecting you to be home this early...is

something wrong?' Kirsten asked, dry-mouthed with fright at the tension in the air.

'Mabel's mother took ill and she's staying the night with her. Where have you been?' Her father's harsh-featured face was ruddy with angry colour and his sharp eyes bright with suspicion.

'I went for a walk…I'm sorry—'

'If I'd been here you'd not have been idling away your time,' he growled. 'What have you been up to?'

Kirsten was rigid. 'Nothing.'

'You had better not be, girl,' he warned her, closing a powerful hand round her thin forearm with bruising force. 'Now, go and make my dinner. Then we'll study the Lord's Book and we will pray for you to be cleansed of the sin of idleness.'

When Angus Ross had stomped out of the kitchen Kirsten rubbed her aching arm with a shaking hand. She was trembling. Her father had never raised a hand to her in anger. She told herself that she had no reason to be so afraid of the older man. It was true that his temper was violent. And in a rage he ranted and raved and stormed up and down in a very frightening manner, but he had never yet become physically abusive with her—or indeed anyone else. So why did she get the feeling that that was in the process of changing?

CHAPTER TWO

FOUR days later, Shahir sprang out of bed at three in the morning and stalked into the luxurious *en suite* bathroom to take another cold shower. A more primitive male might have believed he had been bewitched by an enchantress no human male could resist, but Shahir told himself no such comforting tales.

As the cooling water streamed down over the heated length of his bronzed, muscular body, he groaned out loud in furious frustration. Never before had a woman disturbed Shahir's sleep. But something about Kirsten Ross had fired his imagination to new erotic heights of creativity. The very idea of her as his mistress had become a sexual fantasy he could not shake. Even while he slept his disobedient brain rehashed their brief meeting into an intimate encounter of a wildly uninhibited if unlikely variety that appealed most to the male sex. His inability to control his own subconscious mind infuriated him.

Resting his arrogant dark head back against the cool stone surround, he thought about Faria instead. It was rare for him to indulge himself with reflections about what could not be, for he knew how pointless it was to lament the inevitable. Faria, with her laughing dark eyes and compassionate heart, could never become his wife. Although Faria and he were not related by blood, Faria's mother had briefly acted as Shahir's foster mother when he was very young. And Shahir's religion forbade the marriage of a man to his foster-sister.

He had not known what love was before the day he had glanced across a courtyard at an interminable wedding and seen a very pretty brunette entertaining the children with magic tricks. Faria had grown up while he'd worked abroad, and she had trained as a teacher. He hadn't even recognised her. On the last occasion he had seen her she had still been a little girl.

While Faria had been brought up in the knowledge that Shahir was her foster-brother, *he* had barely heard the matter mentioned. Shahir was royalty, and all too many people claimed to have a connection with him. And, having enjoyed a brief period of intimacy with the royal family in the aftermath of tragedy, Faria's parents, who had never been socially ambitious, had soon returned to their quiet lives. Meeting her as an adult, Shahir had immediately recognised that Faria was exactly the kind of young woman he wanted to marry. In that very acknowledgement the damage had been done—even before he could appreciate that he had mistakenly set his heart on a woman who rightly regarded him as an honorary brother.

Was his nature innately perverse? Shahir asked himself now, his lean strong face shadowed by a dark frown. Although he would not mention his lust for Kirsten Ross in the same sentence as his unspoken admiration for Faria, he could not avoid registering that once again he was guilty of desiring a woman who was forbidden to him. Even that vague similarity disturbed him. In another sense it also challenged him, for Kirsten Ross was by no means out of reach.

Perhaps, Shahir reflected in exasperation, he had become too careful—too fastidious in his refusal to let his libido rule him. Almost certainly he was suffering from the effects of too much sexual denial, and the most effective cure for the foolish fantasies assailing him in the middle of the night would be a welcoming and hopefully very wanton woman.

And he knew exactly who was most likely to qualify in that department. Lady Pamela Anstruther, his nearest neighbour at Strathcraig, invariably acted as his hostess when he entertained at the castle. The arrangement suited them both. Pamela was clever and amusing, a strikingly attractive widow with champagne tastes, struggling to get by on a small income. Shahir respected her honesty and her survival skills. Pamela had never hidden the fact that she wanted him, and that sentiment would not complicate the issue.

At morning break, later that same day, Jeanie frowned at Kirsten. 'You look like you're sickening for something,' she scolded. 'You have dark shadows under your eyes. Aren't you sleeping properly?'

'I'm fine…' Uneasy with telling even that minor lie, Kirsten dropped her head. Several disturbed nights of sleep had left their mark on her face, and she was ashamed of her inability to get the motorcyclist out of her head. Time and time again their encounter would replay in her memory, and when she went to sleep her dreams took over. The disturbing and horribly embarrassing content of them she would not have shared with a living soul.

'Is something wrong at home?'

'No.' Kirsten chewed tautly at the soft underside of her lower lip before finally surrendering to the pressure of her curiosity and saying, as artlessly as she could contrive, 'There was a guy riding a motorcycle up our way last Friday afternoon. I think he was staying at the castle…'

'There's always a bunch of new faces staying in the service wing.' The other woman's attention was concentrated on the large scone she was liberally spreading with butter. 'I bet it was that old tubby guy with the pigtail. You know…the one here to write a history book about the castle. Someone told me that either him or the photographer arrived on a motorbike, dressed like a Hell's Angel.'

'He doesn't sound much like the man I saw.' Kirsten focused on Jeanie's scone, which was being cut into tiny slices so that the pleasure of eating it could be extended. 'He was young, and he looked like he might have originally come from another country—'

'Oh…*him*!' Jeanie's eyes lit up like a row of winning symbols in a fruit machine. 'That'll be the Polish builder working on the stable block. Tall, dark, tanned, super-fanciable?'

Kirsten nodded four times in eager succession, like a marionette.

'I saw him on a motorbike in the village on Saturday night.' Jeanie gave her an earthy grin. 'You've got a pair of eyes in your head at last, have you?'

Kirsten had flushed to the roots of her hair, but could not restrain the all-important question brimming on her lips. 'Do you know if he's married?'

'Kirsten Ross—you shameless hussy, you!' Jeanie guffawed with noisy appreciation. 'No, he's not married. That was checked out by an interested party on his first day. No wonder you're away with the fairies this morning. I spoke to you twice and you didn't notice. Did you get talking to him? I hear he speaks great English. Did you fall madly in love at first sight?'

Kirsten was squirming with embarrassment. 'Jeanie! I

was out for a walk and we only spoke for a minute. I was just being curious.'

'Course you were…' Jeanie was merrily grinning at the prospect of what she saw as entertainment. 'Right, with your face getting off with that builder will be no problem—but somehow I think that getting past your dad is likely to be the biggest challenge.'

'So it's just as well that I'm not thinking of trying to get off with anyone!' Kirsten whispered in feverish interruption. 'Look, please don't go talking about this, Jeanie. If my dad hears any gossip about me he'll go mad! He does not have a sense of humour about things like that.'

'Kirsten…' Jeanie leant across the table, her plump face arranged in lines of sympathy. 'I don't think *anyone* would repeat gossip about you to your father. Since he had that row with the minister and the church elders and left the congregation folk have been very wary of rousing his temper.'

Kirsten jerked her head in mortified acknowledgement of the point.

When the housekeeper signalled her from the doorway, she was glad of the excuse to leave the table and go and speak to the older woman. Offered the chance to work extra hours to cover for a sick colleague, Kirsten accepted gratefully and phoned her stepmother to say that she would be late home.

It was a welcome distraction to be sent to a section of the castle that was new to her. The extensive service wing had been converted to provide state-of-the-art office facilities and a conference center, as well as accommodation for the constant procession of tradesmen and businessmen who visited the remote estate in a working capacity.

Unfurling a floor polisher in a corridor, Kirsten hummed a nameless snatch of music below her breath. *He* was from Poland; a builder from Poland. Had she imagined that upper class accent? But then from whom had he learned the language? Perhaps that had influenced the way he spoke? Suddenly she wanted to know everything there was to know about Poland. Her own ignorance embarrassed her.

At the same time she didn't really know whether she was on her head or her heels. Why on earth was she thinking about a man she would never see again? He worked outside; she worked inside. The castle was huge, the staff extensive. In all likelihood they wouldn't bump into each other again unless he sought her out—and why would he do that? She had shouted at him. Of course if she was the shameless hussy Jeanie had teased her for being she would seek him out for herself. Only thankfully she wasn't. But the thought of never laying eyes on him again made her tummy feel hollow, and filled her with the weirdest sense of panic.

Without warning the floor polisher was switched off, and she straightened from her task in surprise.

'Look, miss. We're having a very important meeting in here, and that machine's damn noisy…couldn't you go and clean elsewhere?' a young man in a suit demanded angrily.

'Yes, of course,' Kirsten muttered, cut to the bone.

Another man appeared behind him, and murmured with glacial cool, 'Don't let me hear you address another member of staff in that tone or in that language again.'

'No, of course not, Your Highness,' the first man framed in dismay, his complexion turning a dull dark red at that cold rebuke.

Kirsten had stopped breathing when the second male

emerged into view, for he was taller, broader and alto-gether more impressive in stature. Her entire being was wrapped in the sheer challenge of recognition: it was the man on the motorbike. But she could not believe that it could be the same person for he looked so very different, in a formal dark business suit the colour of charcoal: sophisticated, dignified, the ultimate in authority.

Belatedly she registered the significance of the title the younger man had awarded him and incredulity sentenced her to shaken stillness. The guy she had met on the hill above the farm was the Prince? Prince Shahir—the enor-mously rich owner of Strathcraig and its ninety-odd-thousand acres? Surely that was impossible? *This is my land,* he had said, but she had assumed he was joking. How could she have possibly guessed that a young man, casually clad in biker leathers, might be so much more than he seemed?

Refusing to allow herself to look back at him, she be-gan to reel in the cable of the floor polisher. Her hands were all fingers and thumbs, and clumsy with nerves. She seized a hold on the weighty machine, in preparation for carting it off to a less contentious area, but her perspiring palms failed in their grip and it toppled back on to the ground again, with a noisy clatter that made her wince in despair. She was supposed to be silent and invisible around him, she recalled in steadily mounting frustration. Was she supposed to abandon the polisher and just run?

'Let me help you with that...'

'No!' Kirsten yelped in horror, when she raised her head to find him standing over her, and she backed away in panic, hauling up the polisher before the lean brown hand he had extended could get anywhere near it. 'Sorry...'

Moving as fast as she could with the unwieldy machine, Kirsten hurried away and sped through the first set of fire doors. For a split second Shahir hesitated, a frown of annoyance and surprise at her behaviour pleating his brows, and then he strode after her.

'Kirsten…' he breathed, before she could reach the next set of fire doors.

Unnerved by the unfamiliar sound of her name on his lips, Kirsten whirled round. She was breathing heavily, her lovely face pink with the effort of carting the cleaner with her. 'You're not supposed to speak to me!'

'Don't be ridiculous,' Shahir retorted crisply.

'I'm not being ridiculous! What do you want from me? An apology? Right, you've got it. I'm sorry I told you off for riding that bike like a maniac. I'm sorry if I interrupted your important meeting…OK, Your—er—Highness?' And, with that almost pleading completion, Kirsten continued to back away, until she hit the doors with her behind, then twisted round and quickly made her way through them.

Shahir followed her at speed, and long before she could draw near the next set of doors he spoke and arrested her in her tracks. 'No—don't move one further step,' he murmured, with a quietness that was misleading; every syllable of that warning somehow contrived to bite into her like a whiplash. 'When I'm speaking to you, you will stand still.'

Kirsten groaned. 'But that's against the rules!'

Shahir vented an unappreciative laugh. 'What rules?'

'The household rules. People like me are supposed to vanish when you appear—'

'Not when I'm trying to speak to you,' Shahir asserted in dry interruption.

'But you're going to get me into trouble… Nobody

knows we've even met, and I don't want to be seen talking to you.'

'That's not a problem.' Shahir opened the nearest door
and thrust it wide. 'We'll talk in here.'

Kirsten sucked in a steadying breath and walked into
an empty meeting room furnished with a polished table
and chairs. 'Why do you want to speak to me?'

Shahir thought he had never heard a more insane question. Any man between fifteen and fifty would have
wanted to speak to her. Her head was bent, her face half
turned away from him, her spectacular hair tied back. But
nothing could hide the silken shine of that pale hair, the
stunning perfection of her profile or the flawless clarity
of her complexion. Nor could a dreary overall conceal
the fluid, willowy grace of her highly feminine figure.

But on another level her sheer lack of vanity and her
naivety shook him. He had never had to pursue a woman
before. Even without his encouragement women gave
Shahir a great deal of attention. Many were so enthusiastic that he had to freeze them out with a façade of cold
formality. Others were more subtle, but equally obvious
in their eagerness to demonstrate their availability to him.
If he showed even the smallest interest to the average
young woman she would fall over herself to respond to
him and roll out the welcome mat.

'Why did you tell no one that we had met?'

Kirsten focused on his superb leather shoes. 'I wasn't
supposed to be on the hill.'

'Why not?'

Kirsten continued to study his feet with fixed attention.
She did not know what to say. She did not want to admit
that her father policed her every move, and the alternative
of lying was anathema to her.

Her seeming defiance challenged Shahir. 'I asked a question.'

A sudden rush of frustrated tears burned the back of Kirsten's eyes, and she threw her head up, green eyes blazing at his persistence. 'I wasn't supposed to be there because my father doesn't like me going out without his permission. I was also reading a magazine, and he won't allow anything like that in the house!'

'I apologise. I should not have pried,' Shahir acknowledged in a tone of regret that he should have embarrassed her. 'But I was curious.'

The thickness in her tight throat would not allow her to swallow. The slight rough edge to his rich, dark drawl feathered down her spine as if he had touched her. Obeying a prompting she wasn't even aware of, she glanced up and was entrapped by brilliant dark golden eyes. 'I was curious about you too...'

Shahir tensed, the honest admission challenging his self-discipline. But he knew that it was his fault—for he had crossed the line and brought down a barrier by getting too personal. He was her employer, he reminded himself fiercely. She had accompanied him into a room where they were alone because he was her employer and she trusted him. What sort of a man would take advantage of such a situation? It did not matter that the attraction between them was mutual. It did not matter that the awareness made the blood pound through his veins like a war drum beaten with intent. That was a cruel trick of fate and not to be acted on.

'When we met, you mentioned damage to your father's field,' Shahir said with flat determination. 'I have had the matter investigated.'

Kirsten simply nodded. That he should have approached her for such a reason made complete sense to her, although she was surprised that he had bothered. She could not take her eyes from his. Never had she been so tense. Her back hurt with the strain of her rigid stance. Her breath was coming in little fast, shallow bursts, her lips were slightly parted, and there was a knot low in her tummy that was tight enough to make her feel uncomfortable. And yet it was a kind of discomfort that was in the strangest way enjoyable.

'It has been established that someone working here at Strathcraig has been biking over that land. He has now been made aware of his mistake and it won't happen again. My estate manager will call on your father to tell him that the damage will be made good at our expense.' His deep rich voice had been husky in intonation as Shahir surveyed her with shimmering intensity, for the more she looked at him the more aroused he became, and it took every atom of his will-power to remain business-like and distant.

'Oh…' Kirsten framed abstractedly.

His bright gaze narrowed, for it was a challenge to believe that she had not been paying attention to what he had said. 'What did I just say?' he heard himself ask in the sizzling silence.

'Something about the field…' Her answer was uneven in tone and she was leaning almost infinitesimally closer. The soft peaks of her breasts had stirred into straining tightness beneath her clothing and she was hugely conscious of that tingling sensation.

'You really aren't listening.' An instinctive charge of masculine satisfaction lanced through Shahir. He liked the fact that she couldn't concentrate around him. He loved it that she was barely breathing. In fact all of a sudden he felt like a marauding pirate on the loose, for his desire for her was primal in its force. He wanted to lift her into his arms, spread her over the table and ravish her glorious body with the kind of exquisite pleasure that would enslave her for ever.

His slow-burning smile hooked Kirsten like a fish. A split second later she found herself wondering what it would feel like if he pressed that beautifully moulded mouth of his down on hers.

It was only then that she realised what was the matter with her, and she was shocked by her own ignorance. With difficulty she dredged her gaze from the burning hold of his and lowered her head. She was appalled that she had been standing there yearning for his touch like the brazen hussy Jeanie had teased her for being. How could she not have guessed immediately that she was attracted to him?

'I'd better get back to work,' she mumbled, half under her breath, but her legs refused to move her in the direction of the door.

'That's not what you were thinking,' Shahir murmured thickly.

His insight shattered her. 'No, it wasn't…'

'So what were you thinking about?' Shahir persisted, his voice husky and low, so intent on her that he could see his own reflection in her dilated pupils.

Kirsten trembled, both frightened and wildly exhilarated by the charge in the atmosphere. Her body felt unbearably taut and sensitive. She could not take her eyes from him for a second.

'Tell me…' Shahir pressed thickly. 'I trust you not to lie to me.'

The revelation of the desire that held her on the edge of painful anticipation had brought down her barriers. She was still in shock. 'I was wondering what it would feel like if you kissed me…'

Shahir muttered something in fierce Arabic and then closed his lean strong hands over hers to ease her slowly closer. He was on automatic pilot, his blood rushing through his veins like a runaway juggernaut, and although at the back of his mind caution was shouting to be heard his sheer hunger slammed the door on that warning voice. 'Let me *show* you...'

His beautifully shaped mouth came down on hers. His kiss was hard and hungry and demanding, but somehow not quite hard enough to satisfy the terrible yearning that was flaming up from the very depths of Kirsten's being. A low moan sounded in her throat and she closed her arms round him, stretching up on tiptoe to intensify their contact. Her hand slid up from his shoulder to sink its fingers into the ebony luxuriance of his hair, and spread there to hold him to her.

She was in the centre of a storm, and it was whipping faster and faster around her. Excitement had dug feverish claws of need into her quivering length for the first time, and unleashed a wildness she had not known she possessed. Nothing mattered but the potent feel of his lean, powerful body against her softer curves, the crushing strength of his arms and the glorious taste of him.

When he parted her velvety soft lips with his tongue and delved deep into the moist tenderness within the sensual shock of that tender assault roared through her. She shivered violently, a muffled little cry escaping her. She was so caught up in what she was experiencing that the sound of a voice on the inter-office call system made her flinch and gasp in surprise.

That intervention in Arabic had the same effect on Shahir as a bucket of cold water, and he had faster reactions. He lifted his tousled dark head, spared one glance for the dazed expression on her exquisite face, and immediately released her from his hold. Caught unprepared, she stumbled and almost fell. Instantly he reached out to steady her again with careful hands.

Breathing shallowly, she backed away into the cold support of the wall behind her while she made a great effort to get her brain back into gear. The confusion created by the sound of the foreign language being spoken on the call system did not help.

'What is he saying? What is it?' she muttered feverishly.

'My PA is informing me that someone has arrived to see me,' Shahir breathed, not quite evenly.

The silence hung around them, suspended, heavy with uneasy undertones. Kirsten could not meet his eyes. Indeed, she could not bring herself to look at him at all. With a sudden moan of unconcealed distress, she sped past him to yank the door open, and she fled as though an avenging angel was in pursuit of her.

Shahir drank in a deep, shuddering breath. Every natural instinct urged him to go after her and apologise for what had transpired, but his staff were already looking for him and Kirsten was obviously upset. It would be foolish to risk a scene that would attract adverse attention to her and increase her embarrassment. What the hell had got into him? He was furious at his loss of control, and could not work out how it had happened. It was as though his libido had hit an override button that had switched off all moral restraint.

Waiting in the elegant reception hall, Lady Pamela Anstruther tapped an impatient foot. Through the glass insert in the fire doors she watched a breathtakingly beautiful blonde girl emerge pell-mell from an office along the corridor. The doors flipped back noisily one by one until the youthful blonde finally rushed past her in tears.

A minute later Shahir came out of the exact same doorway, a forbidding reserve stamped on his devastatingly handsome features.

The attractive brunette's calculating gaze hardened and veiled as she angrily considered what she had just seen and came up with the most likely explanation.

Kirsten stared at herself in the cloakroom mirror. Her green eyes were raw with guilt and shock. Her lips were red and slightly swollen, and tingling. Her body felt hot and tight and wickedly different. Shame engulfed her in a terrible drowning flood. Prince Shahir had been talking gravely about the damage to her father's field. She remembered the way she had been looking at him while he spoke and she wanted to die on the spot. He had asked her what she was thinking about because he had noticed that she wasn't listening properly. Only a very bold woman would then have told him that she was wondering what it would be like if he kissed her! How much more obvious an invitation could a woman give a man? It had been the provocative equivalent of telling him outright that she fancied him. Inwardly she cringed. She was to blame for what had transpired because she had tempted him into touching her.

Finding an empty office, she got on with the job of emptying the bins and dusting and vacuuming. But, as hard as she tried, her response to that kiss kept on coming back to seize hold of her thoughts. In her whole life it had never occurred to her that a man could make her feel like that, and she was shattered by the passion that had lurked undiscovered inside her until that moment of revelation. She was even more devastated by the excitement and pleasure she had felt in his arms. He was a stranger, she didn't even know him, and yet she had found him irresistible—had been so lost in the delight of it that he could have done anything he wanted to her! She felt even worse that it had been him and not her to call a halt to their intimacy.

It was a relief to finish for the day. The staff locker room was very quiet because her usual shift had finished hours earlier. Buttoning her jacket, Kirsten crossed the coach yard to her bicycle. A man who had climbed out of an opulent sports car a few yards away was staring at her in a way that made her feel uncomfortable, and she dropped her head and quickened her step.

'Hold on a minute...' the man urged as she reached for her bike. 'Let me have a proper look at you.'

A bewildered frown denting her smooth brow, Kirsten focused on the tall, thin man in jeans approaching her. 'Sorry...were you speaking to me?'

'You are stunning...' He walked slowly round her, staring at her from every angle with frowningly intent eyes. 'If you're photogenic as well, I can make you the discovery of the decade!'

'I don't know what you're talking about.' Detaching her bike from the stand, Kirsten began to wheel it swiftly away.

'Look, I'm Bruno Judd.' The man hurried after her. 'You may well have heard of me—I *am* an internationally acclaimed fashion photographer. I don't act as a modelling scout in the normal way, but you're very eye-catching and I'd like to take some photographs of you.'

'No, thank you.' Eager to get rid of him, for she thought he was a weirdo, Kirsten climbed on to her bike in haste.

'Did you hear what I said?'

'Please leave me alone!' she muttered fiercely, and pedalled away, leaving him standing staring after her with an air of disbelieving annoyance.

CHAPTER THREE

'I WANT you to find out where Kirsten Ross is working today and I want to speak to her in private. Arrange it, but do so with the utmost discretion,' Shahir instructed his most senior PA, who concealed his surprise at the order with difficulty and bowed out of the room.

Alone again, and restive, Shahir studied the pink roses in the vase by the window. He let a fingertip stroke gently down over the satiny smooth petal of a single perfect bud and thought of the ripe flavour of Kirsten's lips, and the subtle scent and softness of her skin, and swore under his breath almost simultaneously. Her passion had surprised but enthralled him, but he would not allow his thoughts to linger on that fact.

Pamela Anstruther knocked and entered with a suggested guest list for the house party to be held at Strathcraig the following month. Her china-blue eyes met his and she gave him a playful smile, tossing her head so that her glossy brown hair bounced on her shoulders. Her heart-shaped face was very pretty. She was small and curvaceous, and the low-necked summer dress she wore displayed the plump fullness of her breasts and was tight enough to make it obvious that she was wearing the bare minimum of underwear.

He smiled, but the smile was perfunctory and not encouraging—he didn't want her. Indeed, the racy brunette's pert and provocative style was so blatant in comparison to Kirsten's more natural charms that Shahir was repelled.

At that moment Kirsten was seated with a group of other employees on the rough area of grass that lay behind the coach yard. It was hot, and a couple of the young men had removed their shirts. Kirsten hugged her knees and studied her feet—for, having been raised to cover as much of her own skin as possible, she was ill at ease when other people stripped.

'Do you like to go for walks?' the dark-haired man beside her asked quietly.

Her face flamed as the Polish builder addressed her again. He had come over to sit beside her, and everybody had stared, and now he had started to make conversation. She could feel Jeanie's expectant glare like a blow torch on her profile. 'I don't go out very much,' she muttered in a stifled voice, feeling guilty for wishing he would go away and leave her alone.

'Why didn't you make more effort with him?' Jeanie demanded when the lunch break was over. 'I dropped a hint or two on your behalf with one of the guys working with him.'

'Oh, Jeanie…*no*!' Kirsten gasped in mortification.

'Well, I thought you fancied him.' Annoyance was making the other woman sound sharp. 'And why wouldn't you? I wouldn't say no.'

'He's not the guy I met on the hill,' Kirsten cut in abruptly.

'He's *not*?' The redhead frowned, the sharp edge fading from her voice. 'Maybe the lad you met wasn't staying at the castle and was just passing through.'

'Maybe so.' Kirsten hoped that would be the end of Jeanie's attempt to establish the identity of the mysterious biker.

'You'll have to stop being so shy and awkward around men. I mean, don't take this the wrong way, Kirsten—'

her companion sighed '—but you're hopeless. When you won't look at a guy, and then you give him the silent treatment, he thinks you're not interested and that's that. He won't come back for a second helping.'

Kirsten went back to cleaning windows in the long gallery. Every so often she spared the baby grand piano at the foot of the vast room a reflective glance. Would she still be able to play? It had been years since she had had the opportunity. In any case, she wouldn't dare touch any valuable antique at the castle without permission.

Her mother had been a music teacher before her marriage, and had ensured that her daughter had grown up an accomplished pianist. Occasionally Kirsten had stood in for the regular organist at church, but when people had complimented her on her skill her father's face had begun to darken with disapproval. Inevitably Angus Ross had decided that the playing of music was frivolous, and an exercise in vanity, and soon after that the piano had been sold. Her invalid mother had been heartbroken. That was the day that Kirsten had determined that somehow, some way, she would own a piano again and play it every day—for hours at a time if she so chose.

A door opened off the gallery. A dark, stocky man in a business suit waved a hand at her to attract her attention and addressed her in accented English. 'I have dropped a tray…may I please have your assistance?'

Kirsten almost laughed at the drama of that announcement, but she hurried into the room he had indicated, well aware that some of the carpets were extremely valuable. Mercifully only a few pieces of china had fallen on to the wooden floor. Nothing appeared broken, and just a small pool of liquid needed mopping up.

Wielding a cloth from her trolley of cleaning utensils, she proceeded to get on with the task. The man had already departed, and she rested back on her heels for a moment to appreciate her surroundings. She was in a gracious sitting room, with a beautiful plasterwork ceiling, picked out in pretty shades of lemon and green. Fresh flowers and comfortable sofas as well as an open fire offered a warm welcome. However, the presence of a cheerfully burning fire in the month of June made her smile. She could only be in a room that *he* retained for personal use.

Kirsten had begun to listen with interest to the occasional facts that other more informed staff let drop about Strathcraig's wealthy owner. Apparently, even in summer, Prince Shahir liked fires to be lit in the main reception rooms. He did not like the cold.

A door in the corner of the room opened just as Kirsten was getting ready to wheel her trolley out again. Shahir appeared in the doorway. When she saw who it was, she lost every scrap of colour in her cheeks as her eyes travelled from the top of his handsome dark head and down the magnificent length of him to his polished loafers. He looked so gorgeous her mouth ran dry.

'I hope you will forgive me for setting up this meeting,' Shahir murmured levelly, his dark golden eyes absorbing her tension and her pallor.

Her brow pleated. 'You set it up? I don't understand. I was called in here because some china had been dropped...'

His strong jawline clenched. 'I suspect that was merely an excuse to allow me this opportunity to talk to you again in private. I had to see you, to offer you my sincere apologies for my behaviour when we last met. What I did on that occasion was inappropriate and wrong.'

Kirsten was stunned by that forthright declaration. 'But I—'

'You must not attach blame to yourself in any way,' Shahir asserted.

Kirsten knew that such an admission of fault could not come easily to him. In fact she could see the strain of the occasion marked in the tautness of his superb bone structure and the brooding darkness of his gaze. He was a very proud man. Yet he had still gone to the trouble of arranging this meeting so that he could express his regret. She was hugely impressed by the reality that he had not allowed his pride to hold him back. Neither his great wealth and status nor her far more modest position in life had deflected him from his purpose. Even though it would have been much easier for him to forget the incident, he had listened to his conscience and acted on it without hesitation.

'But I was at fault too.' Kirsten lifted her chin, her eyes green as emeralds above the delicate pink that overlaid her cheekbones as she made the admission.

'No. You're very young. Innocence is not a fault,' he murmured in gentle disagreement.

As Kirsten gazed up at Shahir he remembered how she had looked on the hill, with her wonderful silvery pale hair cascading over her shoulders. It was a dangerous recollection, for it awakened the hunger he had rigorously repressed. He gritted his teeth, incredulous at the effect she had on him. He was not a randy teenage boy, living in a world of erotic fantasy. He was a man in full control of his own needs.

'I—'

'I know you would not wish your presence here with me to be noticed and remarked on,' Shahir cut in smoothly. 'It would be unwise for us to linger here chatting.'

Feeling unmercifully snubbed and put back into her place, Kirsten dropped her head and grabbed the trolley.

'I don't like to see you engaged in such heavy work,' Shahir breathed in a driven undertone. 'You do not look strong.'

A startled laugh fell from Kirsten's lips and she glanced back at him, green eyes dancing with helpless amusement. 'I'm as healthy as a carthorse—but I suppose I shouldn't tell you that because it's not very feminine to say so!'

Shahir studied her exquisite face for several taut moments before veiling his gaze. He removed a business card from his jacket and crossed the room to extend it to her. 'If you should ever be in a situation where you need help of any kind, I can be reached at this number.'

Mastering her surprise, she accepted the gilded card from his lean brown fingers. He wasn't flirting with her. His tone and expression were serious and above reproach. The sudden awareness that she was longing for him to flirt with her, touch her and kiss her, shook her rigid. Ashamed of a craving that now felt more wrong than ever after what he had just said, she crammed the card into the pocket of her overall. Hot tears were prickling at the back of her eyes because she suddenly felt unbearably sad.

'Thanks...' she managed tightly, and went back to cleaning windows without another word or look.

Early the following week she was cycling home when the rear tyre of her bike went flat. She had no pump with her, and groaned out loud when it started to rain heavily. Even though she wheeled the bike at as fast a pace as she could contrive she was still soaked through to the skin within minutes.

When a big car drew up beside her and the window went down, she peered at it in bewilderment.

'I'll give you a lift.' It was Shahir, his lean strong face firm with determination.

It bothered her that she could not think of him as Prince Shahir, and discomfiture made her reluctant to get into his limousine. His chauffeur, however, had already received his instructions from his employer, and the bike was removed from her hold and wedged without further ado into the vehicle's large boot.

'Honestly—you shouldn't have stopped. I could've walked home fine… I'm so wet I'll make a mess of your car…' Kirsten was gabbling nervously as she climbed into the rear of the sumptuous car. But she fell suddenly silent and flushed to the roots of her dripping hair when she realised that Shahir was not travelling alone.

'Pamela Anstruther,' the dainty brunette seated beside him said chattily. 'And you're…?'

'Kirsten Ross, ' Kirsten filled in shyly, well aware of who the other woman was.

After all, Pamela's ancestors, the Drummonds, had built Strathcraig and lived there for a couple of hundred years. Unfortunately for Pamela, however, her father's debts had forced the sale of the estate while she was still a child, and the family had moved down to London.

'You're very wet. Take this…' Shahir passed Kirsten a pristine white handkerchief in a graceful gesture. Wet, her hair was the colour of gunmetal, and accentuated the dramatic symmetry of her oval face.

Kirsten pushed a sodden strand of hair off her cool brow and dabbed awkwardly at her rain-washed face. Only then did she dare to steal a glance at him, doing so with as much guilt as though it was a forbidden act.

Her eyes, as luminous as jewels, collided unwarily

with his narrowed dark golden gaze, and her heartbeat increased as if someone had punched a switch. 'Thank you…'

'It was nothing,' Shahir murmured politely, lush black lashes semi-veiling his spectacular eyes.

Her soft pink lips curved into a helpless smile of appreciation.

Pamela Anstruther coughed, and Kirsten instantly dragged her attention from Shahir. Realising that she had been caught in the act of staring, Kirsten turned cherry-red and dropped her head.

'Prince Shahir mentioned that you're on the cleaning staff at the castle,' Lady Pamela remarked brightly. 'You look like a very capable young woman. Do you think you could manage work that was a little more testing?'

'I hope so…but this is my first job.' Kirsten was already looking anxiously out of the window to see where they were, not wanting the limo to take her right to the door of her home. Her father would almost certainly make a fuss about her having accepted a lift.

'Oh, I've just had the most wonderful idea!' Lady Pamela carolled. 'Why doesn't Kirsten help me to organise the party at the castle?'

Kirsten's attention settled back on the brunette in astonishment. 'Me…?'

'Why not? You could run errands for me, and handwrite the invitations. It would be run-of-the-mill stuff— nothing you couldn't handle.'

'I'd love to help.' Kirsten was thrilled by the prospect of doing something other than cleaning.

Lady Pamela rewarded her with a smile. 'I really *love* acting as the Prince's social hostess, but there is a lot of work involved and you could be really useful to me.'

'I'm not sure the housekeeper would be willing to spare me, though.'

Kirsten wanted to look at Shahir, who had said nothing throughout this exchange. But why should he be interested? He might be her employer, but she was at the bottom of a large staff pyramid and she was not so naive as to believe that he had any firsthand knowledge of the castle's domestic arrangements. He paid others to take care of such practicalities, and no doubt Pamela Anstruther was quite free to pluck a junior member from the lower ranks if it suited her to do so.

The limousine came to a halt. Kirsten glanced out of the window and froze, her face draining of colour: her father was glowering on the doorstep, his ruddy face rigid with dour disapproval.

'Oh, dear, who's the nasty old codger?' Lady Pamela asked with an appreciative giggle. 'Ye olde farm labourer?'

Kirsten had already risen to leave the car. The quip mortified her, but she was not surprised that her father's scowling stance had roused such amused comment.

Shahir's attention rested on Angus Ross's aggressively clenched fists. His measuring gaze was cool and his jawline squared. He vacated the limo only a step in Kirsten's wake. As she hovered in obvious apprehension while her bike was being unloaded, Shahir introduced himself to her father. Prompted by Shahir's careful courtesy, Pamela awarded the older man a gracious wave of acknowledgement from the limo. Kirsten was intensely relieved to see her parent's anger banished by the attention he had received from his landlord.

'So the Prince has got that harlot working for him,' Angus Ross commented with an unpleasant laugh when he went back indoors. 'The nerve of yon woman, waving at me like she's the queen! She's hoping to wed the Prince and get the castle back into her family, but she's wasting her time. He must know she's a greedy trollop!'

'Aye, I'd think so. They say he's no fool,' Mabel, a thin-faced woman in her early fifties, agreed with sour enjoyment. 'Before that husband of hers died Lady Pamela had one man after another staying up at that lodge with her! Naturally Sir Robert left her next to nothing on his death.'

'It was God's judgement on her,' the older man pronounced with satisfaction.

Kirsten fondled Squeak's greying ears and wished that her father and her stepmother would be a little more charitable about other people. There were few secrets in so small a community, and she knew the brunette's history too. A good ten years had passed since Pamela had married Sir Robert Anstruther, a wealthy businessman more than twice her age. Pamela had returned to the glen that had once belonged to her family but spiteful tongues had been quick to suggest that she was an unscrupulous gold-digger.

For years Sir Robert had owned an old hunting lodge in the glen, which he had used as a holiday home. Keen to take up full-time residence there, Pamela had renovated and extended the lodge. And while her husband had continued to spend most of his time in London, she had often entertained friends at their highland home. When the older man had died, the gossip had become even more malicious after it became clear that Sir Robert had left the lion's share of his worldly goods to the children of his first marriage.

Kirsten, however, believed that Pamela Anstruther deserved the benefit of the doubt. The other woman had seemed perfectly pleasant to her, and, after all, nobody that Kirsten had heard spreading scandal had ever seen any definitive proof that the lively brunette had been an unfaithful wife *or* was a gold-digger.

'I'm really not interested in being photographed,' Kirsten proclaimed impatiently, four days later, when she was waylaid in the quadrangle that lay behind the service wing.

Jeanie, her hands planted on her ample hips, released a belly laugh at the look of incomprehension on Bruno Judd's thin mobile face. 'Mr Judd, if you knew Kirsten's dad you'd know better than to ask her to model for you in a miniskirt! I'm her friend, and even I haven't seen her knees or her elbows—so what chance do you think you have?'

'You don't understand what an opportunity I would be giving her. There is nothing offensive about my request either. I hate to see potential talent going to waste,' the older man argued in growing frustration. 'Kirsten might have what it takes to become a famous model—'

'Might!' Jeanie emphasised with rich cynicism as the two women walked on, and then she dropped her voice to a whisper, 'Do you think he could be for real?'

Kirsten shrugged. 'Who cares? When I leave Strathcraig it'll be to go to college, so that I can get a better-paying job. I'm not going to waste my time chasing some stupid pipe dream. I bet only one in a thousand girls who want to be a model actually gets to be one.'

'You're too sensible,' the redhead scolded. 'How's it going with Lady Posh?'

'Don't call her that...she's been very nice to me,' Kirsten protested uncomfortably.

'Odd, that, don't you think...when everyone else says she's a total bitch?'

'I think they're being very unkind.'

Ignoring Jeanie's unimpressed snort of disagreement, Kirsten mounted the stairs to the suite Pamela Anstruther used when she was staying at the castle. Kirsten had spent two of the past four days working for Pamela, and she was enjoying the chance to get a break of a few hours here and there from her usual duties. She had answered the phone, run messages and organised the mess on Pamela's desk. She had also unpacked and ironed the other woman's clothes and tidied her room. Pamela treated her more like a casual friend than an employee and Kirsten couldn't help wanting to please her.

A dark frown of disapproval stamped on his lean, powerful face, Shahir watched Bruno Judd finally abandon his attempt to recapture Kirsten's attention as she crossed the quadrangle. There could be no mystery as to the source of the photographer's interest, and Shahir was concerned by what he had seen. The older man was not known for his scruples.

As Shahir turned away from the window, wondering whether or not he should intervene, Pamela Anstruther telephoned to request an immediate meeting with him.

A few minutes later Shahir rose from behind his desk to award the highly strung brunette his reluctant attention. 'What *is* the problem that you prefer not to discuss on the phone?'

Pamela winced. 'It's rather delicate. I'm afraid a piece of jewellery has gone missing from my bedroom.'

Shahir looked grave. 'The police must be called.'

'I don't want to upset the staff by involving the police. Really, the brooch isn't worth very much!'

'Monetary value has no bearing on the matter. I will not tolerate theft.'

'But it is still possible that I have mislaid the stupid thing. Let's not inform the police yet. I'll ask Kirsten to search my suite for it.'

'As you wish.' For an instant Shahir wondered why she had chosen to approach him before an adequate search had been conducted. 'Is the guest list complete yet?'

'Almost. Why don't you join us for coffee today?' Pamela suggested brightly. 'We could make it a working break.'

On the brink of refusal, Shahir hesitated. 'In thirty minutes, then.'

Kirsten was troubled when Pamela told her about the brooch, because she knew that when anything of value went missing everyone who had entered the castle would come under suspicion. 'Of course I don't mind looking for it.'

'Do this room now,' the brunette instructed. 'Then, when the Prince arrives, you can go next door and search my bedroom. Thank you so much. Let's hope you can find it for me.'

Kirsten was down on her hands and knees on the carpet when she heard the deep dark sibilance of Shahir's drawl carrying through from the adjoining reception room. Her throat thickened. She sucked in a jerky breath. No matter how hard she tried not to, she thought about him a lot. Not thinking about him sometimes seemed an impossible challenge, for the instant she relaxed her mental vigilance her thoughts would immediately race back to him again.

Her fingers curled round something small and she looked down in bemusement to see the small brooch that had been lying on the carpet.

'I found it... Oh, sorry!' Kirsten came to a paralysed

halt in the doorway when Shahir sprang upright at her entrance. 'I'm sorry. I didn't mean to interrupt you.'

'My goodness—don't mind that. You found my brooch?' Pamela hurried over to examine it. 'I don't believe it! I went over every inch of that room before you arrived this morning. Where was it?'

'On the floor by the dressing table.'

'But that's *impossible*!' The brunette was frowning in apparent astonishment. 'Of course I'm very grateful not to have to call the police, but I don't understand how I could have missed seeing it there.'

'It happens. Congratulations, Kirsten.' Shahir's calm intercession stole both women's attention.

Kirsten's bewilderment at the other woman's attitude evaporated from her mind when she let herself look at Shahir properly for the first time. Meeting his brilliant dark golden gaze, she felt her tummy muscles clench, and she could barely breathe for excitement. She studied him, feverishly absorbing every tiny facet of his appearance: the way the sun coming through the window behind him found light in his cropped black hair, the amazing bronze clarity of his eyes, the hint of a smile that stole the gravity and reserve from his darkly handsome features. He was so very tall that she wouldn't be able to look down on him even if she were to acquire and get to finally *wear* high heels, she thought abstractedly

'Yes, I'm very grateful.' Pamela Anstruther treated Kirsten to a bright smile of approval. 'Could I have a word with you outside, please? Please excuse us, Your Highness.'

Mystified by the request, Kirsten followed her out into the corridor.

'I just had to get you out of there.' The smaller woman dealt Kirsten a scornful appraisal that bore no resemblance to her usual sweetly sympathetic approach. 'You haven't got a clue, have you? You were seriously embarrassing Prince Shahir and making a fool of yourself. Don't you know better than to gape at the man like a stupid schoolgirl?'

Aghast at the unexpected attack, Kirsten stared at the other woman, and then swiftly lowered her shaken gaze. Her stomach rolled with the nausea of extreme mortification. She was appalled that she had let herself down to such an extent that her behaviour had attracted attention. How could she have been so foolish?

But almost as quickly a spirit of defiance stirred within Kirsten. While she would humbly accept full responsibility for a mistake, she felt that there was some excuse for her lack of composure in Prince Shahir's radius. It was very hard not to be madly aware of the one and only man who had ever kissed her. And, also in her defence, hadn't he stared at her too? For just as long? Was anyone about to slap *his* wrist and rake him down for the same offence?

'Of course I noticed that you had a giant crush on the Prince that day he gave you a lift home. That's hardly surprising. He's a staggeringly handsome man. But I'm quite sure that you don't want people to start laughing at you.'

Kirsten lifted her chin. 'I don't think I made myself ridiculous.'

The cold china-blue eyes narrowed at that quiet comeback. 'I suppose you think I've been brutal, but someone had to warn you for your own good. Look, why don't you finish early today and go home?'

Kirsten did nothing of the sort. One or two of her coworkers had been less than impressed by her newly flexible employment conditions, and she deemed it wisest to head down to the staff locker room in the basement, don her overall and finish up her usual shift.

While she worked she began to revise her initial favourable impression of Pamela Anstruther. Perhaps she had been a touch naive about the imperious brunette, she acknowledged ruefully. Whatever—it was obvious that she had really angered Pamela. She could only suppose that there was truth in the rumour that Pamela was interested in Shahir, for she felt there had been no need for Pamela to humiliate her to that extent.

When she was pulling on her jacket to go home she was told that the housekeeper was looking for her.

'You're wanted back in the service wing,' the older woman informed her ruefully. 'I did say it was your finishing time, but you're to wait in Reception there.'

Kirsten was dismayed by the news. Was she in trouble about something? Had she so annoyed Lady Pamela that the brunette wished to dispense with her assistance? She had barely sat down in the waiting area when one of Shahir's office staff appeared and indicated that she was to follow him. She was mystified right up until the moment she was shown into a large, imposing office and saw Shahir poised by the window.

Her fine facial bones tensed beneath her smooth porcelain skin. She felt torn apart: she wanted to see him and she didn't want to see him. Her heart hammered behind her breastbone and her green eyes feasted on him while her brain battled against any acknowledgement of the sheer charisma of his dark good looks. But every time she saw him she was afraid it would be the last time, and that honed her interest in him to a desperate edge.

For the merest instant Shahir pictured her slender loveliness spread across his bed, her beautiful hair loose in silver streamers he could bury his fingers in, that luscious soft pink mouth ripe and ready for his. Even as he angrily suppressed that unwelcome flight of erotic fancy his body punished him with a raw masculine response. He was the descendant of a long line of fierce warrior ancestors, and self-denial figured nowhere in his genes, he acknowledged grimly. His hunger for her might be in his blood, like a primitive fever, but he was proud of the fact that only regard for her wellbeing had persuaded him that this meeting was necessary.

Shahir rested steady dark bronze eyes on Kirsten. 'You must be wondering why I wished to see you?'

'Yes.' But the familiar frisson of sweet tightness was already curling in Kirsten's tummy and she was deliciously tense. He had sought her out again, and that pleased her so much she felt that she was floating ten feet off the ground. If she smiled she knew she might not be able to stop. For the first time ever a sense of her power as a woman was flaring through her, and it shook her to recognise that questionable feeling for what it was.

'I saw Bruno Judd trying to speak to you.' His husky dark drawl was incisive in tone. 'I understand that it is not the first time he has approached you, and I was concerned.'

His explanation took Kirsten entirely by surprise. She came down from her fluffy mental cloud of irresistibility with a resounding crash and her face flamed. She could not credit that she had been so vain as to assume that he had had a more personal motive for wishing to see her.

In an effort to conceal her discomfiture, she burst straight into speech. 'He wants to take some photographs of me. He thinks I might have what it takes to become a fashion model.'

'Very well. It will be my pleasure to ensure that you aren't troubled by Mr Judd again,' Shahir informed her.

Kirsten was already feeling silly and hurt, and mortified to the depths of her soul, and his high-handed statement of intent sent her flying from miserable awkwardness to angry defensiveness. What right had he to assume
that she would not be interested in Bruno Judd's proposition? She might be forced to accept her father's tyranny
at home, but she saw no reason why anyone else should
be allowed to take decisions on her behalf, or assume the
right to tell her how she ought to behave.

'But Mr Judd isn't troubling me,' Kirsten countered in
flat rebuttal. 'And if he was I could quite easily send him
about his business if I wanted to.'

'But of course you must want to.' Shahir's conviction
of his own greater wisdom came as naturally to him as
breathing. 'You're not streetwise enough to survive in the
modelling world. The fashion industry is tough and cor-
rupt, and it favours very young teenagers. Judd won't
stand by you if your face fails to make his fortune. He
is a talented photographer, but he has few scruples.'

Kirsten flung up her head, green eyes sparkling like
polished gemstones. 'I can look after myself!'

Shahir studied her with dark eyes cool as ice. 'Please
don't raise your voice to me. I do not tolerate imperti-
nence.'

Kirsten lowered her lashes. She was as chagrined as a
child who had been told off and sent to stand in the
corner, and embarrassment struggled with resentment inside her. Her usually even temper sparked. She felt angry
with the world in general. And the knowledge that she
could not speak freely and could not even risk raising
her voice had the same effect on her as a gag. The silence
fairly sizzled with undertones.

'My only wish is to protect you from exploitation,'
Shahir murmured with icy gravity.

That cold intonation of his wounded her even more. 'Maybe I'm more streetwise than I look.' Hurt and bitterness rose like a tide inside her, and she stole a burning emerald glance at him. 'Maybe I *want* to take my chance at becoming a model!'

Her mouth ran dry as she met the smouldering gold of his appraisal. Anticipation coursed through her in a wicked helpless surge: she felt as though her heart was in her throat, choking her with its accelerated beat. A dam-burst of tension was pooled up inside her, like oil waiting for a flame to ignite it.

'Naturally that must be your decision.' And with that unemotional assurance Shahir opened the door for her departure.

As a victory it rang hollow for Kirsten. She bent her head, her hands clenching in on themselves with unbearable tension, her emotions erratic. She dimly understood that in teaching her to want him he had destroyed her peace of mind. By making her crave what she could not have he had made her vulnerable to pain and dissatisfied with what she had. Even being polite to him was a challenge for her. Indeed, something very like hatred powered the deep sense of rejection she was experiencing. Never in her life had she felt so bereft. But she walked away with her head held high.

On the way out of the building she checked her pigeonhole and found a magazine. Brand-new, and still sealed in its wrapper, it was the same publication that Shahir had found her reading on the hill. She did not know how, but she was immediately convinced that he was responsible for the anonymous gift.

Just as quickly she found that she was able to see their recent encounter in another light. He had been worried about her. She might not have appreciated the way he chose to express his opinion, but the very existence of his concern touched her. Her anger evaporated. Suddenly the world no longer seemed such a cold and hostile place. His indifference would have wounded her intolerably. But the mysterious arrival of the magazine allied to his attempt to protect her felt comforting. In that lighter mood, she headed home.

She knew something was wrong the instant she entered the kitchen. Her father was seated alone at the table, his weathered face set like granite. 'You're late. What have you been doing?'

'I was held up at work.' Uneasily conscious of the older man's accusing stare, Kirsten struggled to behave normally. 'That's all.'

'Don't lie to me!' Angus Ross slammed a clenched fist down on the worn table and made her jump. 'That man Judd was here!'

Wholly unprepared for that announcement, Kirsten stared at her father in bewilderment. 'Mr Judd came…*here*?'

'Thanks to you, he brought his dirty suggestions into my home.' Kirsten flinched back a hasty step as the older man reared upright and came towards her. 'What have you to say about that?'

'I had nothing to do with him coming here,' she protested in a nervous rush, appalled by the news that the photographer had been foolish enough to approach her father in the hope of winning his support. 'I have no idea why he would have done such a thing—'

'He thought he could fool me into letting you go down to London with him!' the older man snarled. 'He showed me pictures of shameless half-naked women. He defiled a God-fearing household with his filth.'

'I'm sorry he upset you, but he's just a pushy man with silly ideas. He doesn't know anything about me.'

'You're lying, girl. He knew where you lived. You told him you'd need my permission to leave home. You put him up to it, didn't you?'

'No, I didn't. He must have asked someone where I lived. I told him I wasn't interested in being photographed. I'm sure he didn't mean to insult you—'

'It's you who's insulted me! You must've encouraged him!' His rage was unabated by her efforts to calm him down.

'But I didn't!'

'You're lying to me and I won't stand for it!'

With that roared declaration, Angus Ross raised a fist the size of a sledgehammer and thumped her.

CHAPTER FOUR

THE next morning Kirsten would have avoided going into work if she could have done. Her cheekbone was bruised and swollen, and she knew that someone was sure to ask what had happened. She also knew that unless she was prepared to report her father to the police she would have to lie.

Had she not turned her head, so that the main force of the blow was deflected, her nose might easily have been broken. She was equally conscious that, having hit her once, her father might just as easily hit her again. Her tummy flipped when she recalled the older man's intractable fury. He hadn't cared that he had hurt her, and he hadn't been ashamed either.

Hearing Kirsten cry out, Mabel had rushed downstairs, and had seemed very much shocked by what she found there. Yet within an hour of that distressing episode Mabel had been laying the blame for Bruno Judd's visit and her husband's violence at Kirsten's door.

Her eyes were hot and scratchy from the silent tears that had seeped under her eyelids the night before. Her father had never been a soft man, but he had not been a brutal one either. In fact he had once been reasonably well-respected in the community and she was deeply ashamed that he had struck her.

Evidently Jeanie had been right to be cynical about the prospects of Kirsten managing to leave home with her father's approval. But the need for her to move out was now a matter of greater urgency, and it was obvious that she would have to plan a secret departure. Unfortunately her cash reserves were still pitifully low. She decided that she would put her name down to work extra hours whenever possible.

'My word…what happened to your face?' Pamela Anstruther asked in a hushed tone of enquiry within minutes of Kirsten's arrival.

'I tripped and hit myself on the edge of a table…I was lucky not to break anything,' Kirsten stated with an uneasy shrug.

The brunette gave her a sympathetic look that was reassuringly empty of suspicion. 'Poor old you. Look, I only need you for an hour this morning. You can tidy my bedroom and then go back to your usual duties when we're done.'

Kirsten repressed a stab of disappointment and resentment. So this was to be yet another day when she did not get to help with the party arrangements. She had always liked to think of herself as ready and willing to turn her hand to most tasks. But the brunette had taught her that there were tasks…and tasks. Pamela always left her room like a rubbish tip, and Kirsten really disliked being used as her personal maid.

His handsome mouth compressed into a hard line, Shahir studied the letter he had received that morning from a cousin. And then, with a sudden bitter laugh, he crunched the item up and tossed it in the bin.

It seemed a fitting footnote to his non-relationship with Faria that he should have learned quite accidentally that the only woman he had ever cared about had just become the wife of another man. He had not even been aware that she was betrothed!

But, owing to the recent death of a relative, Faria's

wedding had been a small, quiet affair, staged at speed to facilitate the bridal couple's departure for London, where the bridegroom had taken up a surgical post.

It had been inevitable that Faria would marry, Shahir acknowledged bleakly, and she was no more out of his reach now than she had ever been. He refused to allow himself to feel unsettled by the news of his foster-sister's marriage. He was strong, not weak, he reminded himself with grim resolve.

An hour later Pamela Anstruther arrived, to collect the corrected guest list from him.

'I think that Kirsten Ross has been up to no good,' she remarked with a suggestive roll of her eyes.

Shahir elevated a cool ebony brow that would have silenced a less bold woman.

Predictably, Pamela continued to talk with animation. 'You see, I did hear a rumour that Kirsten was sneaking out to meet the Polish builder working here. The life she leads, I certainly don't blame her for trying to hide something like that. Unfortunately for her, though, it seems that her nasty old father has got wind of her promiscuous behaviour—'

'I have a strong dislike of rumour and gossip,' Shahir sliced in dryly.

Pamela gave him a sweet smile of apology. 'I gathered that you felt sorry for the girl—that's the only reason I mentioned it. You see, Kirsten isn't looking quite as pretty today as she usually does.'

Shahir levelled unreadable dark eyes on the brunette. 'Get to the point, Pamela.'

'Well, the poor girl looks like somebody punched her in the face, and I suspect her gruesome old dad is responsible.' Pamela watched Shahir and was disappointed by the fact that his lean strong face remained impassive.

'Did she say so?'

'Of course not…she trotted out the old "I tripped" chestnut. But I reckon that her daddy found out that she was doing what healthy farm girls do with a man when they get off the leash!' Pamela vented an earthy laugh that had the subtlety of a brick hitting glass. 'You disapprove of that kind of speculation, but it *is* the most likely explanation—and who could fault her for it? From what I understand she's not allowed any freedom at all, and that's not natural for a girl of her age.'

When the brunette had gone, Shahir released his breath in a measured hiss. He would have a member of his senior staff raise the matter of Kirsten's welfare with the housekeeper. He would ensure that all possible advice and assistance was offered to her. What need was there for him to involve himself in any more direct way?

But was it true that Kirsten was involved with a man? That she had already acquired a name for being promiscuous? Distaste assailed Shahir. What did he really know about Kirsten Ross? Regard for her good name had prevented him from discussing her or her background with anyone. He had assumed that she was an innocent, and vulnerable. But now he was remembering her passion in his arms and wondering whether it had, in fact, been the response of a more experienced lover.

Could he have been mistaken? He could hardly tell the difference on the basis of one stolen kiss, he conceded abstractedly. And why the hell was he even thinking about such a thing? Virgin or wanton, she was still forbidden to him.

On the other hand, he was one hundred per cent weary of the nonsense attached to his expressing an honest and entirely proper concern for the wellbeing of an employee. Why should he have to act unseen, through intermedi-

aries? Why should he have to tiptoe around the sensibil-
ities of his staff? If Kirsten had been assaulted, why
should he not check that shocking fact out for himself?
In the palace where he had grown up he would not have
hesitated to do so.

After all, his entire upbringing had been geared to the
need for him to feel personally responsible, protective
and compassionate towards more vulnerable human be-
ings. He had picked up that lesson at a very young age.
He had been taught that no person and no problem should
ever be considered beneath his notice or too small to
warrant his individual attention. An honourable man did
what was right, regardless of appearances!

Without further ado, he accessed the housekeeping rota
on the computer, to establish where in the castle Kirsten
was likely to be. He did not allow it to occur to him that
until very recently he had not even known such rotas
existed, or where they could be found.

Kirsten was brushing the polished floorboards of the long
gallery. For once she had little appreciation for the mag-
nificence of her surroundings. The prospect of going
home that afternoon was already filling her with a sense
of dread that overshadowed her every thought. What sort
of a mood would her father be in?

'Kirsten…'

At the sound of her name she jumped, and the brush
fell from her nerveless fingers and hit the floor with a
noisy clatter. Her pale head flying up, she focused in
surprise on Shahir, who had come to a halt about twenty
feet away.

In one glance he saw the fear she could not hide and
the purple discolouration that marred one side of her face.

His outrage at what he saw slashed right through his cool reserve.

'What has happened to you?' he breathed, his long stride bringing him to her side within seconds. 'Did your father do this to you?'

His candour thoroughly disconcerted her. All morning she had been horribly aware of the sidelong looks and whispered comments behind her back, but only Pamela Anstruther had dared to question her. 'No—I don't know where you got th-that idea,' she stammered, nervously evading his frowning scrutiny. 'I stumbled and fell against a table.'

Shahir lifted a lean brown hand and let a gentle forefinger brush the edge of the bruise that stood out in livid contrast to the porcelain perfection of her skin. It enraged him that she had been brutalised. Her home life was clearly appalling, and her predicament could not be ignored. Yet if she was allowed to enter staff accommodation at the castle would her father leave his daughter there in peace? Shahir doubted that it would be so simple. Such a man would not easily surrender control over his own flesh and blood.

'I know that is nonsense,' he asserted with quiet conviction. 'You cannot look me in the eye and lie.'

At his touch, which felt like a delicious caress, Kirsten had stiffened in astonishment. Until that moment she had not known that a man could be so gentle. Her emotions felt like dynamite on a hair trigger. Keeping the lid on them demanded every ounce of her self-discipline. His attention, his very interest in her, was already having an intoxicating effect on her. He was so close that she could smell the faint and already surprisingly familiar scent of his skin. Soap? Some expensive shaving lotion? For an instant it was all she could concentrate on: the aromatic

mystery of that clean, rich tangy preparation that somehow made her tingle inside her clothes and want to move
closer still.

'I'm not lying,' she mumbled in belated response, feeling bereft because he had withdrawn his hand again.

'You have been hurt, and that is not acceptable under
any circumstances. No one has the right to inflict injury
on you, not even a parent. I must know the truth,' Shahir
persisted steadily. 'Without your trust, I cannot help you.'

'You couldn't help me anyway!' The involuntary protest erupted from Kirsten, and stinging tears flooded her
eyes and overflowed, her unhappiness unconcealed.

'In that you are wrong.' Years of rigorous royal training prevented Shahir from attempting to comfort her by
closing his arms round her, but he had never been more
tempted to break the rules. He recognised that it had been
very unwise to tackle her on such an emotive matter in
a public area of the castle. 'But this is definitely not the
place for us to talk about it.'

'We can't talk anywhere!' Kirsten gasped.

In disagreement, Shahir curved a purposeful hand to
her spine and guided her along to the door that lay at the
foot of the gallery. Beyond that solid mahogany barrier
lay his private quarters, maintained solely by his personal
retinue, where nothing short of fire or flood would lead
to an interruption. His bodyguards, who had been deeply
unhappy when their royal charge moved out of their sight
and hearing, greeted his reappearance with pronounced
relief.

Shahir swept Kirsten past them into the vast sitting
room. 'I need you to calm down and tell me what happened to you yesterday.'

'I *can't* tell you...' A stifled sob thickened Kirsten's
declaration.

Shahir reached for her hand to draw her to him when she would have turned away in an effort to conceal her distress. 'Loyalty to one's family is always a most admirable trait, but in this case your personal safety is more important. What happened yesterday could happen again, and you could be more seriously hurt.'

'But it's my own fault…I brought it on myself!' Kirsten protested guiltily.

'How could it be your fault?'

'If I'd let you scare off Bruno Judd this wouldn't have happened! But I was mad with you because you interfered, and I thought it was none of your business,' Kirsten admitted shakily, her green eyes glimmering with tears of regret.

'Hush….' Murmuring soothing words in Arabic, Shahir sank down on the arm of a sofa and reached for her other hand in a reassuring gesture. 'Don't be upset. How is the photographer involved in this?'

'That stupid man found out where I lived and called round to introduce himself to my father,' Kirsten volunteered. 'He must've thought that he could persuade Dad that there was no harm in his wanting to take photos of me.'

'Judd visited your home?' Shahir frowned, his lean, powerful face intent on her.

'And showed Dad pictures of ''shameless h-half-naked women''!' Kirsten quoted, with a hysterical edge to her shaking voice. 'Can you imagine anything more guaranteed to cause offence? My father was waiting for me to come home. He was in a real rage—'

'No more…stop remembering.' Shahir rested a forefinger in gentle reproach against her quivering lower lip while wondering how it was that the livid bruise should only seem to accentuate her fragile beauty. 'He will not have the opportunity to hurt you again. I will not allow it.'

'But there's nothing you can do,' she whispered unevenly, her breath feathering in her dry throat.

'On my word of honour, I will protect you,' Shahir swore with fierce resolve, but he knew even as he said it that the easiest way to protect her would be to take her away from Strathcraig.

But how would she survive removed from everything and everyone that she knew?

Why should he not look after her? an insidious inner voice queried. Why should he not take her to his bed? What did she have here? What would he be taking her from? Poverty and misery. At the very least he would make her happy. In fact he was convinced he had the power to make her deliriously happy.

Suddenly madly aware of the silence surrounding them, and of his proximity, Kirsten muttered guiltily, 'I shouldn't be here with you.'

Brilliant dark golden eyes flared over her tear-streaked face and held her uncertain gaze with arrogant force of will. 'But you want to be with me...'

It was a fatal statement, for the barrier she had attempted to raise crashed down again. She did want to be with him—and if even he knew that, why should she pretend otherwise? She was in the mood to rebel, and was already asking herself why she shouldn't for once do as she wanted.

The heat of his appraisal sent hot little flames of anticipation twisting and curling through her slender length. The tension was excruciating. She felt as if her own heartbeat was thundering in her ears at a faster and faster pace, making her dizzy and breathless. In an almost infinitesimal movement she shifted closer to him.

Shahir picked up on that feminine encouragement with a hot-blooded masculine appreciation powered by the raw physical charge of his arousal. His mounting conviction that she was not quite the innocent he had believed readily put to flight any lingering thread of restraint. Spiky black lashes semi-cloaked his narrowed gleaming gaze as he focused on the luscious pink fullness of her lips. 'I want you.'

'Do you?' Her breath was feathering in her throat. She was taut with anticipation. He sprang fluidly upright and reached for her with a strength and assurance that exhilarated her. Splaying his hand to the soft curve of her hip, he urged her up against his big powerful frame. Crushed to the hard, muscular heat of his strong body, she trembled. He bent his handsome dark head and captured her parted lips with devastating hunger.

The searching flicker of his tongue against the roof of her mouth made her shiver and gasp. She angled her head back so that he could plunder the tender interior. His lips were warm and skilled, and unbelievably sensual. One kiss left her craving the next with helpless impatience.

'You are as eager for me as I am for you,' Shahir growled, taking her swollen pink mouth again, with a demanding urgency that she found irresistible. Lifting her, he brought her down on the hard cradle of his thighs. Deft fingers released the zip on her overall and pushed the garment from her shoulders to free her from it.

'Oh…' Her dazed green eyes flew wide open as he let an exploring hand travel over the pouting thrust of her small breasts beneath the dark blouse she wore. The straining tips of her tender flesh tightened and swelled within the cups of her bra.

'Oh…' Shahir mimicked her with a sensual mockery

that felt as unreal as everything else that had so far happened between them.

But, unreal or otherwise, she was already in thrall to the insistent demand of her own body. He pressed his knowing mouth to the tiny pulse-spot below her ear and nuzzled the sensitive skin there. Startled by the resulting leap of sensation, she clenched her fingers convulsively into his sleeves.

'I've never been into discomfort.' With that husky declaration, Shahir gathered her up into his arms and stood up as if she weighed no more than a china doll. 'And as a rule I prefer to make love in bed—although I am not saying that I could not be tempted by a more adventurous venue.'

Bed? Never had a single word seemed more graphic in its connotations!

Kirsten tensed in dismay, for she had not thought beyond the defiant act of enjoying kissing and getting close to him. But Shahir chose that exact same moment to bend his well-shaped dark head and let his tongue dip between her parted lips in a provocative and incredibly enervating sneak invasion. Kirsten melted like ice cream on a hot griddle, and did not surface from the grip of that all-encompassing loss of rational awareness until she found herself standing positioned between his splayed thighs while he sat on the edge of a bed. He had already undone the clasp at the nape of her neck to release her hair from confinement.

'I desired you the first time I saw you,' Shahir confessed, skimming lean brown fingers slowly through the shimmering fall of her pale silvery blonde hair. 'Every time I saw you from that moment I desired you even more…'

She was so tense that her knees wobbled beneath her. 'Truthfully?'

'Though you do not seem aware of the fact, you are extraordinarily beautiful.'

The clear green eyes clinging to his lean dark features clouded with sorrow. Her hand fluttered up to touch the ugly bruise. 'Not today, I'm not...'

Shahir enclosed her thin hand in a firm grip. His dark golden eyes were as bright as the heart of a fire. 'Today you seem even more beautiful to me.'

A laugh that wasn't a laugh at all was wrenched from Kirsten. Her eyes glimmered and her throat worked. Suddenly she was tipping herself forward and claiming his perfectly moulded mouth for herself, with passionate urgency. He unbuttoned her blouse, and the fastener on her trousers, tugging her down on to his lap to extract her with smooth expertise from her clothing while his kisses held her imprisoned.

'You wear so many clothes,' he censured thickly, one hand knotted in her silky hair to tip her head back so that his marauding mouth could trace an enterprising trail across the sensitive skin of her throat.

As her bra fell away, and cooler air brushed her nipples, Kirsten went rigid with shock and closed her hands over her exposed breasts.

Shahir stilled and tipped back his handsome dark head. He swept her up and settled her back against the pillows, straightening again by the bed to look searchingly down at her. 'I assumed that you were no stranger to sex. If I am mistaken, tell me, and you can leave without reproach,' he murmured tautly. 'I don't seduce virgins.'

Her lashes lowered over evasive green eyes. She hugged her knees to her chest, silvery fair hair falling round her like a screening veil. Her thoughts were in turmoil.

Growing up in Angus Ross's home had made her familiar with constant disappointment. Virtually everything that might give her pleasure had been denied her. Now she wanted Shahir more than she had wanted anything in her whole life. His candour gave her a choice. If she told him the truth, he would send her away from him, and she could not face that conclusion.

'I'm not a virgin.' she muttered in a rush, telling the lie before she could think through what she was doing and lose her nerve.

Shahir was very much in the mood to be convinced. Though in every way that mattered she was different from every other woman he had ever known. 'You seem very shy...'

Kirsten focused fixedly on her bare toes. 'Do you have a problem with that?'

He surveyed her delicate profile with smouldering golden eyes full of appreciation. 'No.'

'Then could you please close the curtains?'

Taken aback, Shahir raised a questioning brow. 'Do you only make love in the dark?'

Kirsten nodded vehemently.

Torn between a desire to laugh and an uneasy stab of tenderness that discomfited him, Shahir hit the buttons that closed the blinds and the curtains.

In the sudden darkness, Kirsten slid nervously off the bed. Her toes tangled with the garments scattered on the floor and she fell over her own feet.

Winded, she lay there until Shahir picked her up, saying, not quite steadily, 'You may make love in the dark, but I don't think you have night vision.'

'Obviously not...' The lamps on either side of the bed

lit up and she blinked rapidly at the sudden restoration of light.

His attention zeroed straight down to the prominent rosy nipples that crowned the pert thrust of her breasts. 'Why would you seek to hide such perfection?'

He closed his hands over hers before she could cover herself again, and backed her down on to the bed with masculine purpose. He cupped and stroked the small tempting mounds, and let his thumbs rub over the straining crests. She gasped as liquid heat snaked down to her pelvis and pooled there to form a knot of intense physical longing. He lowered his dark head and let his hungry mouth play over the distended pink buds.

She moved trembling fingers into the dense luxuriance of his cropped black hair. 'Shahir…'

'I like the way you say my name…' With a groan of reluctance he vaulted upright and proceeded to strip off his suit jacket and his tie.

Passion-glazed eyes widening, Kirsten watched him pull open his shirt to reveal a bronzed and muscular slice of chest. Off came the shirt, to reveal the hard contours of hair-roughened pectorals and the corrugated flatness of his stomach. He was all male, from the satin-smooth strength of his broad shoulders to his narrow waist and long, powerful thighs.

As he shed his well-cut trousers and stood revealed in black boxers she could feel her face starting to burn with hot colour. She wanted to look and she didn't want to look. The jersey boxers left little to the imagination, and her imagination was already running riot. He peeled them off, and for a split second she stared in apprehension, then quickly shut her eyes tight in mortification. There was too much of him, she thought in a panic. There was no way he was going to fit her, or she was going to fit him.

'I'm not shy,' Shahir confided, quite unnecessarily.

'I know,' she mumbled, not looking within six feet of him and scrambling below the sheet.

'But I find your shyness appealing,' he murmured in a surprised tone of discovery. 'It's very sexy.'

'Oh…'

'Oh…' Shahir mocked again, thrusting back the sheet.

Dark eyes slumberous, he leant over her and ran a slow, possessive hand over the silken swell of her breast down over her quivering tummy to the taut line of a lissom thigh. He let his tongue lash a tantalising pink peak and the breath hissed in her throat as she flung her head back, her back arching.

The knot of desire low in her belly twisted tighter. He parted her legs with gentle resolve, explored the silver curls that screened her feminine mound, and traced the slick smooth folds at the heart of her, where she was tender and swollen. She couldn't stay still. Her hips jerked and shifted on the bed. The hunger was back with a vengeance, fiercer and stronger than she could stand.

'Oh…*yes*,' Shahir breathed with raw satisfaction against her reddened mouth, and he eased a finger into the hot wet welcome that awaited him.

'Please…'

'It's too soon,' he husked.

He toyed with her melting body until whimpers of need were torn from her lips and she was writhing beneath the onslaught of an almost agonising tide of pleasure. Only then did he rise over her and plunge his hard male shaft into the sweet, tight depths of her receptive body. She was aching for him, eager—and completely unprepared for the sudden sharp tearing pain that made her cry out.

Abruptly, Shahir stilled. A lean hand turned her face up to his. Burnished golden eyes clashed with hers, his astonishment unhidden. 'You lied to me? You *are* a virgin?' he bit out incredulously.

Hot-faced, Kirsten shut her eyes tight shut and said nothing.

Shahir gazed down at her in disbelief. Never until that moment had he been aware of just how young she was, and never once had it crossed his mind that she might not tell him the truth. 'Kirsten…'

'Don't stop…' she mumbled, arching up to him in a shamelessly inviting movement that made her face flush with embarrassment. But she couldn't help it; she really couldn't. Somewhere down deep inside her there was an unrelenting throb of desire that was driving her crazy, and she knew that only he could satisfy it.

Torn between anger and a desire that was burning at fever-pitch, Shahir hesitated, his powerful muscles straining with the force of the self-discipline he was exerting over his powerful libido. But, on the edge of withdrawal from the sweet allure of her body, he rebelled against all restraint and slammed back into her with a harsh groan of satisfaction.

She cried out in excitement, sensation rippling through her in heady waves as pain became pleasure. He pushed up her knees, to deepen his penetration, and sank into her over and over again. She abandoned herself to a passion that was pagan in its wildness. He took her to the dazzling heights of sensual ecstasy and a climax of shattering intensity.

Lethargic and happy, stunned by her own capacity for physical enjoyment, Kirsten could barely think straight in the aftermath of her first experience of lovemaking. He held her close, kissed her brow.

She got to revel in that glorious intimacy for perhaps sixty seconds before he pulled back from her again.

At a moment when Kirsten was still floating on mental clouds of bliss, Shahir looked down at her, his stunning dark golden eyes cool and intent. 'Don't ever lie to me again.'

Wholly unprepared for the dynamic verbal condemnation and warning combined in that one pungent sentence, Kirsten gaped at him.

CHAPTER FIVE

'You don't have to make such a fuss about it!' Voicing a spirited defence, Kirsten pulled herself up against the tumbled pillows and hugged the sheet to her bare curves, which suddenly felt sinfully naked and exposed.

'Do I not?' Shahir demanded wrathfully, not backtracking a single inch—indeed, seizing the chance to argue the point with the stubborn resolve that was the backbone of his character.

'No, you don't.' Her discomfiture was pronounced. 'I told a little white lie—'

'There is no such thing!' Shahir tossed back the sheet and vaulted out of bed. 'I said I would not touch you if you were a virgin, and you chose to lie rather than tell me the truth. That was an act of deceit, and unfair to me.'

Taken aback by his cutting candour, and by the aggressive masculinity of his naked bronzed body, Kirsten flushed a deep guilty pink and averted her eyes from his powerful physique. 'It was my choice.'

'But it would not have been *my* choice to destroy your innocence. That was a betrayal of the principles that I respect,' Shahir imparted grimly, striding into the dressing room to gather up clean clothes and then continuing on into the adjoining bathroom.

Kirsten heard the sound of a shower running. She still had a convulsive grip on the sheet. A surge of stinging moisture was washing the back of her eyes and she swallowed the painful lump in her throat. She had acted wrongly, and the punishment for her misbehaviour was coming even faster than she had feared it would. She had surrendered her virginity to a man who didn't want it and who did not feel even remotely appreciative of the fact that she had given it to him because she felt he was special.

In what way was he special now? She crushed back that daunting reflection of her own ignorance when it came to men and tried to concentrate.

But it was a challenge. Here she was, desperate for some reassurance from him, even a little warmth and affection, and he was acting as if she had murdered someone. He had also called her a liar and, while strictly speaking that might be true, she really wasn't in the habit of telling lies. Unfortunately she had been upset, and she was very attracted to him, and somehow those two things had combined to wash away her usual level-headed and honest approach to life.

Shahir reappeared, looking formidably elegant and intimidating in yet another dark and beautifully tailored suit.

Kirsten spared him a skimming glance before fixing her attention on the foot of the bed. 'I'm sorry I lied, but I really wasn't thinking about what I was doing,' she admitted in a small, tight voice. 'Now that I am thinking, I wish I hadn't lied to you.'

His brooding gaze lightened several shades at that acknowledgement, but he was determined to drive home his point that he would not tolerate dishonesty. If, as he planned, she became a semi-permanent feature in his life, it was a lesson she needed to learn. 'Lies damage trust,' he pointed out levelly. 'How long do you think it will be before I am prepared to trust your word again?'

Kirsten wasn't listening to him. Having opened up the box of her own regrets, she was now steadily drowning in them. She not only wished that she hadn't lied to him, but was beginning to wish that she had not slept with him. 'I really just wish this hadn't happened—'

'We are not children, Kirsten. We chose to allow it to happen.'

'There's no need to rub it in! It's the worst mistake I ever made in my stupid life…'

'We were both unwise.' Shahir was struggling to silence his conscience while at the same time telling himself that there was no point in agonising over what could not be altered. He had wanted her. Now he had her—in more ways than one. He would be a liar if he overplayed the show of regret. 'But an apparent mistake may yet be turned into a more positive development.'

'I don't see how…' Wrenching the sheet from its moorings, Kirsten wrapped it clumsily round her and clambered off the bed, her lovely face tight with unhappiness.

She longed to have the ability to close her eyes and magically escape from the scene of their intimacy. Why on earth had she not had the sense to flee while he was in the shower? She felt much too ashamed to look him in the face as she stooped to pick up her discarded clothing, piece by mortifying piece. How could she so easily have disregarded every moral rule that had been drummed into her from childhood? She hardly knew him, and yet she had gone to bed with him. She was shattered by that reality, for in her right mind such an act seemed unthinkable to her.

She could see the sheer, terrifying power of her own emotions had combined with sexual attraction to destroy her self-respect. He had looked at her and he had touched her and all her common sense and self control had vanished. How could she continue to deny that she had feelings for him? Was she infatuated with him? Was she in love? He had haunted her thoughts and her dreams from their very first encounter on the hill. But she did not see that as an excuse for what she had allowed to happen between them.

'Stop this…' Catching her slender hand in his, Shahir gently detached her blouse from the fierce hold she had on it.

'But I have to get back to work—'

'No, you do not.' Shahir pressed her down into an upholstered chair. 'I want you to listen to me.'

'I really do need to get dressed—'

'Look at me,' he urged huskily. 'We are lovers now.'

Kirsten froze, the reminder deeply unwelcome. A flush of pained colour washed her cheekbones. She felt utterly wretched. She linked her trembling hands tightly together and made herself look up at him. 'Why do you have to throw that at me? Don't you think I feel bad enough as it is?'

Shahir dropped down in an athletic crouch so that his brilliant dark-as-midnight gaze was on a level with her. 'You should not feel unhappy about what has happened between us—'

'Well, I do,' she cut in unevenly.

'This could be the beginning of a new life for you.'

Her smooth forehead indented. 'How?'

'Obviously after this you can no longer work here. But I won't let you go home to your father again either. From now on I will make myself responsible for you.'

'What are you trying to say?'

'That you can simply get dressed and walk out into the limo with me and never return here.'

Her lashes fluttered up on bewildered green eyes. 'You're asking me to leave Strathcraig with you?'

Shahir wondered why it was that he was finding it difficult to come to the point. 'I'm asking you to continue being my lover.'

Kirsten sucked in a startled breath and attempted to master her astonishment. 'But—'

'Hear me out before you speak. I have an apartment in London. You can live there until you have had the time to choose a new home, of your own. I'll buy you that home and take care of all your needs.'

Shock was rippling through Kirsten as she understood what he was offering her—shock, and the beginnings of anger. 'You really don't have any respect for me, do you? Is that because I work as a cleaner? Or because I went to bed with you before we even got as far as a first date?'

Disconcerted by the unexpectedly volatile response, Shahir murmured flatly, 'Respect doesn't come into this—'

'I noticed! Well, I may have behaved in a very stupid manner today, but I do know the difference between right and wrong! And I may not be a virgin any more either,' Kirsten conceded with fierce discomfiture, 'but there is no way I'm about to turn into some cheap floozy you keep for sex!'

Shahir sprang upright. 'That is a distortion of the facts.'

'For someone who doesn't like lies you can be very imaginative with the truth,' Kirsten muttered bitterly.

'That could be because I very much want you to become a part of my life.'

'No, you don't!' Her eyes were hot with unshed tears but she was quivering with furious pain. 'You think I'm not good enough for anything but sharing a bed with. That's fine. Don't you dare think I care about that. But feeling as you do about me, you should have stayed well away from me!'

With that emphatic accusation, and almost blinded by tears, Kirsten snatched up her clothes, fled through to the bathroom and slammed shut the door. She would have liked a shower but was afraid of getting her hair wet. Even so, she was desperate to make good her escape and get back to work. Having made do with a hurried wash at the vanity unit, she dragged her clothes on over skin that was still damp.

Who would ever have thought that he would invite her to be his mistress? She must have been all right in bed, she reflected painfully. He would not want a repeat performance otherwise. He wouldn't want to offer her a house either. How could he have dared to talk of her becoming part of his life when it was so obvious that all he was interested in sharing with her was sex? When he would essentially be keeping her in return for the use of her body?

That offer was so horribly humiliating. Yet what else had she expected from him? She had not looked before she had leapt. How could she have any kind of normal relationship with a prince? The enormous gulf between them could never be bridged. That was why she should not have slept with him. Playing by the rules and keeping her distance would have protected her. Now her body had an intimate ache that she knew she would never forget.

She suppressed the sob clogging up her throat. She wanted so badly to relive that wonderful moment of togetherness when he had held her close before it all began to go wrong. But that was impossible.

Her home life had been destroyed by her father's violence. Now continuing to work at the castle would feel equally unsustainable. She did not want to see Shahir again. She did not want to work for him in any capacity either. What had once seemed like honest employment would now feel demeaning, she conceded unhappily. Somehow—and soon—she had to find a way to leave the farm and find another job.

Dragging in a shuddering breath of oxygen, she rested her damp brow against the wooden door and then opened it again.

Shahir was pacing the sitting room, his lean, darkly handsome features taut and grave. A heartbeat after Kirsten's flight from his presence, his intelligence had kicked back in and cold logic had prevailed. His perfectly orchestrated and rational existence had gone off the rails and crashed at spectacular speed. He was a disciplined man, and he was not accustomed to finding himself in the wrong, but he had too much integrity to deny the obvious. In retrospect he was sincerely appalled by his own unscrupulous behaviour.

Had he been more disturbed by the news of Faria's nuptials than he was prepared to admit? He saw that it had suited his purpose to give credit to Pamela Anstruther's sleazy suggestion that Kirsten was promiscuous. And he felt it unpardonable that that slur had made Kirsten seem more accessible and his own desire for her more acceptable. Only now that sanity and clear judgement had been restored did Shahir recognise that *nothing* could excuse his having become intimate with an employee.

Yet even that was not a fair appraisal of his misconduct, Shahir acknowledged bleakly. He had taken unprincipled advantage of a virgin—a naive and vulnerable young woman who should have been able to rely on him for support during a troubled period in her life. Instead he had betrayed her trust, and acted in a way that had

increased her distress. He could not evade responsibility
for the damage that he had caused. And suggesting that
she become his mistress had been an even more distaste-
ful act on his part. He was ashamed, and he knew what
honour demanded of him in restitution.

Kirsten lodged in the doorway like a nervous fawn,
ready to run for the undergrowth at the first sign of threat.
'I'm sorry...I need my overall.'

As she hastened across the room, her eyes screened by
her lashes, and stooped to pick up the garment, Shahir
addressed her. 'Kirsten, I have to talk to you.'

Kirsten refused to look at him. She was holding herself
together, but only just managing, and she would have
died rather than break down in front of him. 'You don't
need to say anything at all. I bet you'll be relieved to
hear that I don't expect to be working here for much
longer. In fact I won't even be living at Strathcraig any
more.'

'I am not relieved to hear those facts. Where are you
planning to go?' Shahir demanded with a frown.

'I have plans.'

'Plans are not enough. Don't allow what happened between us to persuade you into making an impulsive decision. You are suffering a lot of strain right now, and I
am aware that I have made the situation worse.'

Pride brought up Kirsten's chin, and she tossed her
head. 'Actually...I was coping fine until you suggested
that I could enjoy a dazzling future as a whore!'

His superb cheekbones were prominent below his
bronzed skin, and faint colour accentuated the proud slant
of them. 'I will not attempt to defend myself. I should
not have made such a suggestion.'

Flustered by the unexpected admission of fault on his
part, Kirsten found it easier to concentrate on putting her

overall back on, and then she rushed into the tense silence to break it. 'That's all right…forget it. By the way, I never did say thank you for that magazine you got me.'

'What magazine?'

One glimpse of Shahir's mystified expression was sufficient to tell Kirsten that she had made yet another embarrassing mistake. He had not been responsible for leaving that magazine in her pigeonhole—and why on earth had she assumed that he had? Wishful thinking? Her cheeks burned.

'Never mind… Look, we've got nothing more to say to each other,' she muttered hurriedly.

'In that you are mistaken. I owe you an explanation for my behaviour.'

'I don't think so.'

'Please…'

The sound of that unfamiliar word on his lips allied to the terrible strain in the atmosphere made her eyes sting with tears. She could feel his remorse, and it was as sharp as her own. Oddly enough, his regret at what had happened between them hurt her more than his suggestion that she become his mistress.

She stole a brief glance at him from below her lashes. He was breathtakingly handsome. She remembered his mesmerising smile, the golden sheen of his skin against the white bedlinen, the warmth and the feel of him below her fingertips. Guilty pleasure almost consumed her, and a tiny twist of wicked heat sparked.

She tore her attention away from him in deep shame. Why could she not control her mind and her body?

'I will order coffee.' Shahir was determined to bring a more civilised note to the proceedings.

'No…please, let's just get this over with.'

Shahir studied her pale perfect profile in frustration.

Suddenly it was as though she was locked away from him in a place he couldn't follow. Even when she had been forced to look in his direction he had felt as though she could not quite see him.

'I hate to see you so unhappy. Matters may well have gone awry today because we were both too preoccupied with other events in our lives to be thinking clearly.'

Her attention caught, she glanced at him. 'Other events?'

'Your father had struck you, and I...' His beautifully modelled masculine mouth clenched as he steeled himself to make a personal admission that did not come easily to a male of his reserve. 'I too had some reasons to be disturbed. This morning I learned, quite by accident, that a woman who was important to me had become another man's wife.'

Kirsten could feel the blood draining from below her skin. She dropped her head and stared a hole in the magnificent rug beneath his polished leather shoes. His confession had hit her like a body-blow. It had come out of nowhere and he might as well have plunged a knife into her heart. *A woman important to him?* Obviously he was referring to a woman whom he loved. Yet it seemed almost unimaginable to Kirsten that Prince Shahir could have fallen in love and met with rejection.

Yet he had just told her so. He loved someone else. That thought steadily blocked out every other: Shahir's heart belonged to someone else.

The new awareness blazed a burning, wounding trail of pain across Kirsten's very soul. He loved another woman and, unable to have her, had taken Kirsten to bed instead. She had been a stop-gap, a distraction, a consolation prize. She felt sick with hurt and humiliation.

'What's her name?' she asked shakily.

Shahir had not been prepared either for the lengthy silence that followed his admission or for what he deemed to be the irrelevant question. His ebony brows pleated and his answer was reluctant. 'Faria...'

'You didn't need to tell me about her.' Kirsten could not help wishing that he had remained silent, for in telling her the truth he had lacerated her pride and filled her with a hollow sense of anguish.

'There was a need. I'm not in the habit of behaving as I did today. I took advantage of you and I wish to redress that wrong.' His lean, strong face was set in hard lines of resolve. 'In this situation there is only one way in which I can do that.'

'I don't understand. What's done is done.'

'Marry me,' he murmured levelly. 'Marry me and become my wife.'

Kirsten parted her lips to vent a shaken laugh, but no sound came out. Involuntarily focusing on him, she met dark golden eyes as steady as they were serious. 'But that's the craziest thing I ever heard...'

'It is not. This is not a liberal community, and you are not from a home where sex outside marriage is deemed acceptable. Naturally you are upset by what has happened between us, and you have a right to be. In taking advantage of your trust when you were in an emotional frame of mind I acted with dishonour.'

'But to propose marriage to me...' Words failed her.

She was stunned by the turnaround in his attitude. It was, however, beginning to sink in that his conduct towards her must have been very much out of character. Yet that acknowledgement only made her more painfully aware of his love for Faria. He must have been thinking of Faria when he took her in his arms, and that hurt.

'Why not? Sooner rather than later I must marry someone.'

'But surely not just anyone?' she framed shakily.

'You're very beautiful.'

All over again Kirsten felt the ignominy of being valued for her physical charms alone. Indeed, it seemed to her that the looks that had attracted him to her had extracted a high price from them both. He believed that he had wronged her, but she refused to accept that he was at fault and she totally blameless. Had she admitted her inexperience he would not have slept with her. She was responsible for her own behaviour. She had wanted him. Even knowing that what she was doing was wrong, she had encouraged him to make love to her. Now she had to accept the consequences. He was only asking her to marry him because he felt guilty, and she hoped she had enough pride and decency not to take any man on such discreditable terms.

'Let's just forget about all this.' Her strained green eyes locked to his stubborn jawline and rose no higher. 'You don't owe me anything. I'm not holding you to blame. There's certainly no need for you to be offering me marriage.'

'There is every need,' Shahir countered.

'I appreciate the offer. I really do. I don't want to be rude either… But I'd have to be really desperate to marry anyone without love.' Especially a man madly in love with another woman, Kirsten affixed inwardly.

'This is your decision?'

'Yes. May I go now?' she prompted uncomfortably.

'As you wish.'

Shahir watched her hasty retreat from his presence with grim dark golden eyes and a rare sense of incomprehension. He had expected her to accept his proposal.

Indeed, the prospect of refusal had not crossed his mind. He had already been planning the best terms in which to present such an unequal marriage to his father. He should be relieved that would not now be necessary, and that honour had been satisfied without any degree of personal sacrifice. Disturbingly, however, all he could think about was the fact that there was now no way that Kirsten Ross could ever adorn his bed again.

Kirsten had managed barely three steps down the gallery before Jeanie appeared at the far end and gave her a frantic wave.

'I've been looking everywhere for you. Have you been off some place crying?' the redhead asked with rough sympathy. 'Well, guess what? There's a big panic on in the basement. Something valuable has gone walkabout and the staff lockers are being searched. Everyone has to agree to their locker being checked…but can you imagine how it would look if you refused?'

'Like you were guilty.' Relieved that Jeanie had noticed nothing amiss, Kirsten made a determined effort to behave normally. 'What's gone walkabout?'

'Haven't a clue. The housekeeper and her sidekicks aren't telling.'

So much had happened so fast to Kirsten that she felt disconnected from the world around her. In the midst of the noisy chatter of the staff room she sat in a daze, lost in her own increasingly fantastic thoughts.

Suppose she had been insane enough to say yes to his proposal, she was thinking. Would Shahir really have married her? He would scarcely have asked had he not been prepared to do so. Would she have become a princess? Was there the remotest possibility that she might have made him happy? That he might have fallen out of love with Faria and fallen in love with her instead? How low would it be to marry a man who was only asking out of guilt? Very low, or only a little bit low?

When the senior housekeeper, Mrs Cook, appeared, with her thin face set in severe lines, Jeanie nudged Kirsten to attract her attention. 'Now someone's for it...'

'Kirsten...could I have a word?' Mrs Cook enquired.

Silence spread around Kirsten like a pool of poison. Getting up with a bewildered frown, she followed Mrs Cook into her office, where the older woman's two assistants were waiting.

'This was found in your locker.' A sparkling diamond pendant on a gold chain was placed on the desk in front of Kirsten.

'That's not possible...' Kirsten studied the pendant in disbelief. It was familiar to her, for on at least two occasions she had seen it lying in a careless heap on Pamela Anstruther's dressing table.

'We have a witness who says she saw you hiding it in your locker during your lunch break,' Mrs Cook divulged.

Stunned by that announcement, Kirsten immediately endeavoured to argue her innocence.

What followed was the worst experience of her life. She insisted that she had not entered the locker room since the start of her shift. She declared that it was impossible for there to be a witness to an act that had not happened. She had neither stolen the pendant from Pamela's bedroom, nor attempted to conceal it.

The witness, Morag Stevens, one of the two assistant housekeepers, then stepped forward to tell her story without once looking in Kirsten's direction.

When Kirsten realised that nobody was paying the slightest heed to her protests and defensive explanations she became very scared and upset. But within the hour it was all over. She was informed that she was very lucky that Lady Pamela did not wish to have her prosecuted for theft, and she was dismissed on the grounds of gross misconduct. The contents of her locker were packed into a bag and she was escorted out of the castle.

Jeanie was waiting at the courtyard gate for her. White-faced, Kirsten got off her bicycle to speak to the other woman and tell her about her dismissal. 'I didn't do it, Jeanie. I swear I didn't!'

'I'd be amazed if you did. After all, you'd be the first to be suspected, and you'd have to be a right idiot to think you could get away with it!'

'But why did Morag say she saw me put the pendant in my locker at lunchtime? Why would she lie? Why would she do that to me?'

'Maybe she stole it and then got nervous and hid it in your locker? She has access to the pass keys,' Jeanie reminded her. 'But somehow I'd be more suspicious of Lady Posh.'

'Lady Pamela?' Kirsten interrupted in astonishment. 'Why would she have anything to do with the loss of her own jewellery?'

Jeanie grimaced. 'I first smelt a rat when Lady Posh came over all nice and asked you to work for her. She's never been a nice person. But if she did stitch you up, I can't imagine why or how she did it—and I bet you won't ever be able to prove it. She's a clever one.'

Kirsten bowed her head, thinking of all that Jeanie did not know, and all she did not feel able to tell her. Yes, she acknowledged, she had annoyed Pamela Anstruther by staring at Shahir. But that had just been a little thing, hadn't it? It would be fantastical to suspect that Pamela would deliberately set her up to be falsely accused of theft, sacked and discredited. Yet it did not make any more sense to Kirsten that Morag Stevens would have stolen the pendant, only to conceal it in someone else's locker.

Kirsten's head spun when she attempted to come up with a viable explanation for what she had initially assumed had to be a ghastly misunderstanding or a case of mistaken identity.

'What are you going to do?' Jeanie prompted.

A light switched on in the dark turmoil of Kirsten's thoughts: she would make use of that business card and phone Shahir. She seized on the solution like a drowning swimmer. He would not let her be blamed for something she had not done. He would never believe that she was a thief. If he insisted, the matter would have to be more fully investigated and then surely the truth would emerge.

'Your dad will go bonkers if he finds out you've been done for theft,' Jeanie said worriedly.

'It's Friday. I have the weekend to tell him,' Kirsten mumbled, but her stomach was churning at the very idea.

'Kirsten, you can't tell him. You can't take the risk. No offence intended, but your dad can act like a bit of a nutter. Why don't you come home with me?'

The minibus that ferried castle employees back to the village every day was now within sight.

'I couldn't possibly—'

Jeanie gripped her arm for emphasis. 'You can always phone me. You're welcome any time of the day or night. My dad won't mind you staying with us.'

Kirsten got home as quickly as she could. Breathless, she hurried up to her bedroom, removed the small gilded card from below the mattress and hurried back downstairs to dial Shahir's mobile phone.

When Shahir answered the call, she hurtled straight

into speech. Maybe he had already been told about the pendant, but she was praying that he had not and that her version of events would be the first he heard.

'I have to see you…it's urgent.'

There was a brief moment of silence before he suggested that they meet in an hour's time at the viewpoint which lay about half a mile from her home.

She took strength from the fact that his rich dark drawl sounded the same as usual.

His lean, strong face austere, Shahir set down his phone.

CHAPTER SIX

FROM the viewpoint there was a spectacular panorama of the glen of Strathcraig and the mountains. Surrounded by dense forest, the turreted castle looked like a fairytale palace in a sunlit glade. On the valley floor the water of the loch gleamed as still and as blue as a tear-shaped sapphire.

The silence rushed in Kirsten's ears, and then she heard the faint recognisable purr of a car engine climbing the hill. A couple of minutes later the limousine pulled in to the parking area.

Kirsten started to speak before she even got inside the vehicle. 'I know you must be wondering why I contacted you—'

'No. I am aware of what occurred this afternoon.' Shahir rested impassive dark eyes on her, his absolute calm and composure intimidating her. For a moment it seemed as if the intimacy they had shared earlier that day might never have happened.

That cool, level tone made Kirsten lose colour. 'I *didn't* take that pendant.'

Shahir shifted a lean brown hand in a silencing gesture. 'Although I could not condone theft in any circumstances, I do understand why you did it.'

Kirsten stiffened. 'But I didn't do it!

'Kirsten…I myself witnessed what was probably your first attempt to steal from Lady Pamela.'

Totally taken aback by that astounding claim, Kirsten

whispered, 'My *first* attempt? What are you talking about?'

His bronzed profile took on a grim cast. 'I am referring to the brooch that mysteriously reappeared after Pamela had already conducted a search for it. You luckily found it. Possibly you took fright when she so quickly noticed that the brooch had gone missing and you decided to replace it.'

Her brow had furrowed, an expression of consternation blossoming in her candid gaze. 'Are you saying that you thought I was only pretending to have found the brooch?'

'At the time I did not think that. But I do not place great credence in coincidence.' Shahir regarded her with uncompromising cool.

'Neither do I, but—'

'I must be frank. When I learned that the pendant had been discovered in your locker, I recalled the matter of the brooch. Taking those two incidents into consideration, I would find it impossible to accept that you have been falsely accused of theft.'

That unequivocal declaration slammed into Kirsten like a punch in the stomach: she felt sick and she could hardly catch her breath. She did not know why, or even how, but from somewhere she had managed to acquire immense faith in Shahir's ability to divine the truth. Now that faith seemed impossibly naive. She was in shock as well, because his explanation had added another whole layer of complexity to the theme of her presumed guilt. 'You honestly believe that I'm a thief?'

'There is considerable sympathy for your situation. Had there not been, you would have been prosecuted,' Shahir delivered in a flat undertone 'You are living in distressing circumstances, and naturally you must want to leave your home. Carrying out that objective requires money. Only today you yourself informed me that you did not plan to be at Strathcraig for much longer.'

'Yes, but I didn't mean I was planning to steal jewellery to fund my getaway!' Her head was aching. She wanted to scream with frustration and sob with anger and fear and hurt. She felt horribly isolated and misjudged. She had done nothing wrong, yet a plausible case had still been made against her. People thought she had resorted to pilfering because she was desperate to escape her unhappy home life. No doubt her bruised face had made it even easier for some to believe that she was guilty as charged.

'I intend to give you the financial help that you require to leave your home.'

Her head flew up, green eyes suddenly bright as chipped emeralds as furious mortification took hold of her. 'No, thank you. I won't accept money from you!'

'I want to help. It is only right that I should. I may not be able to condone theft, but I can comprehend your desperation.'

Rage was pumping through Kirsten in an adrenalin rush. She did not trust herself to speak. She tried to open the car door, but it remained infuriatingly closed.

'The door is locked as a security measure. What I have said may be unwelcome to you, but I am not your enemy,' Shahir murmured dryly.

Kirsten flung her head back. 'Oh, yes, you are! I trusted you, I had faith in you, and I don't know why! I had this stupid idea that somehow you would *know* that I didn't take that pendant! Instead you're accusing me of having tried to steal the brooch as well. Let me out of this car!'

'Calm down. You are being foolish.'

'No, I'm not!' Kirsten raged back at him, a flush of

pink mantling her delicate features. 'I'm not a thief, and I don't want your wretched charity. Maybe you'd like me to disappear into thin air because you slept with me, but I'll leave Strathcraig under my own steam and in my own good time—and I don't need anything...least of all help...from you!'

Hard dark golden eyes slammed into hers with the efficacy of a missile hitting a direct target. 'Control yourself. That is *enough*.'

He had not raised his voice. He did not need to do so. His intonation carried enough measured force to quell a riot. Quivering with angry distress, Kirsten sucked in oxygen and expelled it again in a shaken surge. She did not want to control her temper. She was afraid that if her anger dimmed her strength would sink with it, for even in the midst of hating him with all her heart she was conscious of the terrible shock and pain of his misjudgement.

'Whether you accept it or not, I care about what happens to you,' Shahir asserted. 'I would not otherwise have asked you to marry me.'

'Your conscience cares, but you don't *really* care!' Kirsten condemned in fierce argument.

'I would like to know that you are safe and unharmed, and there is no guarantee of that in your current environment.' He settled an envelope down on the seat beside her. 'Use it or burn it. The choice is yours.'

'It's great to have more money than sense, isn't it?'

Shahir ignored that childish crack. 'Are you prepared to press a charge of assault against your father?'

'No.' Kirsten shook her head vehemently.

'Then you cannot be protected from him. Have you no relatives who might intervene on your behalf to reason with him, or who might offer you a home?'

Mute, she shook her head again. Her parents had both been only children. 'I have a brother, Daniel. He quarrelled with my father five years ago and left. I don't know where he is. He hasn't phoned or written home since then.'

'Were you close to your brother?'

'When we were kids, but goodness knows where he is now.'

'It might well be possible to have him traced and found, but that would take time. It would seem that your only immediate option is to leave Strathcraig. I am offering you my support to do that.'

'What support? Your cash? You've let me down.' With pained satisfaction, Kirsten watched his angular masculine jawline clench at that condemnation.

'Regardless of what you believe, I am concerned for your welfare. If you leave the glen, you must let me know where you are.'

'Why would I do that when you don't believe a word I've said?' Kirsten flared back at him. 'I am telling you the truth. I am not a thief and I certainly don't require your advice or your money. I'll manage fine on my own, thank you very much! Now, let me out of this car!'

She was rigid with the amount of emotion that she was holding in. She could not bring herself to touch the envelope. She did need money, but not his. To accept even a blade of grass from him would have hurt like hell.

Scrambling out of the car, she trudged back down the hill. She did not look back. She would not permit her thoughts to rest on Shahir, or on the encounter that had just taken place. That would be a severe waste of mental energy. Had she been foolish enough to believe that her handsome prince would come to her rescue, like some guy in a fairy story? Well, now she knew different. Her world had become a very scary place, and the wound he had inflicted with his mistrust was the most raw of all.

All too well aware that she dared not stay within her own home, she made herself think of practical things. She would pack a small bag, because that was all she could carry on her bike. And she would have to take up Jeanie's offer of hospitality—for the night at least. Would Squeak be welcome as well? She knew that she dared not leave the elderly dog behind, lest he become the focus of Angus Ross's thwarted rage.

Kirsten carted the laden tray past tables packed with lunchtime diners and deposited it in the kitchen.

'You shouldn't be doing that.' Donald's kindly face below his thinning red hair was full of concern as he served up another basket of chips. 'You deal with the bills. Stay away from the heavy work.'

Kirsten just nodded, and waited until he was out of view before massaging the ache in her lower back. The diner was always understaffed, and with the other waitresses struggling to cope, Kirsten refused to sit idle behind the till. She was well aware that she was lucky to still have a job.

It was more than seven months since she had walked out of her home, leaving only a brief note of explanation behind. Donald was Jeanie's brother, and he and his wife, Elspeth, had been very good to Kirsten.

The weekend after Kirsten had left the farm, Donald and Elspeth had visited Strathcraig with a trailer to pick up her personal effects. The couple had given Kirsten a lift down to London. To begin with she had rented their spare room, and she had been grateful to walk straight into a job as a waitress at the café that Donald managed.

She had had to work long hours to save up sufficient to put down a rental deposit for a bedsit.

At first she had felt lost in the city. The sheer volume of the crowds and the traffic and the noise had stunned her. She often pined for the wild grandeur of the mountains and the peace and silence of the glen. But from the outset she had refused to look back with regret, and to satisfy her longing for green places she had explored the London parks with Squeak. While she'd focused on the new and bright future she was determined to carve, she had busily searched out information on further education courses.

It had not been difficult to decide that she should set her sights on training as a music teacher. As a first step in that process she had signed up for a couple of evening classes. Although she already held the required qualifications as a musician, she needed to gain exam passes in other subjects before she could hope to apply for a place on a degree course. She had been happy to face the prospect of several years of studying and living on a very low income. In fact she had felt privileged to have the opportunity, and proud that she had the courage to try and get more out of life than her father had been prepared to allow her to have.

In almost every way her future had looked full of promise, and she had worried that it was all too good to be true. Unfortunately her misgivings had proved correct, for she had soon discovered something that had wrecked all her carefully laid plans and made everything infinitely more complicated.

Another waitress began filling ketchup bottles behind the counter. When Kirsten tried to help, Patsy urged her to sit back down on a stool by the till.

'A good gust of wind and you'd fall over,' the older

woman scolded, closing a motherly hand round Kirsten's thin forearm for emphasis. 'You're too skinny to be healthy. When did you last see the doctor?'

'I've always been thin.' Kirsten sidestepped the question, because she had overslept and missed her last appointment. 'Stop worrying about me.'

'I can't help it. You don't look strong enough to lift a teaspoon, and that baby will be here in another few weeks,' Patsy sighed ruefully.

'I'm fine.'

Kirsten turned away to deal with a customer. The swell of her tummy bumped against the counter. The new awkwardness of her body embarrassed her, and she had yet to adjust to her changed shape. Sometimes she would catch a glimpse of her reflection in a shop window or a mirror and she just wouldn't recognise herself.

Indeed, she had already been four months pregnant by the time she'd discovered that the queasiness she was suffering from was the result of something more than a persistent tummy bug.

Truth to tell, she had been desperately unhappy when she'd first arrived in London, and she had fought her misery every step of the way. Night and day she had waged a battle of denial against the male whose image haunted her every waking hour. She had tried to fill all her time with work or study. The strain of that crazy timetable had destroyed her appetite. It had been ages before she even noticed that her periods had stopped. Believing that stress and weight loss were the cause, she had not been unduly concerned. It had only been when the nausea refused to go away that she'd recognised the need to consult a doctor.

Even at that point it had not occurred to her that she might be carrying a baby. In retrospect her blindness seemed utterly and inexcusably stupid to her. After all, she might have been a virgin, but she was certainly old enough and wise enough to be aware that sexual relations could lead to conception. Unfortunately all such rational considerations had been hampered by the simple fact that just thinking about Shahir reduced her to a useless heap of emotional rubble and self-loathing. In an effort to protect herself from destructive thoughts she had suppressed her every recollection of him—and of the forbidden passion they had shared that day.

Only when the doctor's diagnosis had forced Kirsten to look back to their short-lived intimacy had she realised that she could not recall Shahir having taken the precautions that would have protected her from pregnancy.

The prospect of becoming an unmarried mother had made her feel sick with shame—and very scared. And then she had been so angry with Shahir she had boiled with rage. How could he have been so careless with her? While he might seem to be the ultimate in cool control on the surface, she was aware of a wild, reckless streak underneath. She had seen that side of him on the motorbike—and in bed. An electric frisson of awareness ran through her whenever she recalled the scorching golden glitter of his eyes.

Why should Shahir worry if her life was to be wrecked by the burden of single parenthood? Once the baby was born, how was she to work or attend evening class? With a child to care for it would be a much bigger challenge for her to make ends meet and finish her education.

She had thought about phoning Shahir to inform him that he was destined to become the father of her child. But Shahir had called her a thief and, since she had denied the charge, he had to think that she was a liar into the bargain. His uninhibited regret at having slept with her, not to mention his being hopelessly in love with another woman, had not been in his favour either. What pride she had left had revolted at the idea of announcing her pregnancy to a man who would equate her news with catastrophe.

'How's that little dog of yours doing?' Patsy enquired chattily, breaking into Kirsten's troubled thoughts.

'He's still sleeping a lot. I don't take him walking out as much as I did. The vet says he's just old…' Strain edged Kirsten's voice, for she adored Squeak and she was terrified of losing him: he was her last link with her late mother.

When she'd finished her shift, she walked out on to the street. It was cold, and the street lamps cast a yellow glow over the wet pavement. A few yards ahead of her a car door opened and a man climbed out. Light glinted over his cropped black hair, shadow falling over his lean bronzed profile. Then he straightened to his full imposing height and her breath tripped in her throat. Shock froze her in her tracks, wide green eyes welded to his arrestingly handsome face.

'I seem to have frightened you…that wasn't my intention,' Shahir drawled, as smoothly as if they met and talked on a regular basis.

'How did you find out where I was?' Kirsten exclaimed, busily engaged in buttoning her coat in an instinctive attempt to conceal her protruding stomach.

'Ways and means. Are you feeling all right?' Shahir stared down at her, a frown pleating his ebony brows. 'You're very pale.'

'Am I? This light makes everyone look weird,' she gabbled, striving to act normally. 'What are you doing here?'

'I came to see you.'

She folded her arms, discovered her tummy got in the way of what had once been her waist and hastily dropped her arms again. 'Why?' she asked baldly.

'I did ask you to stay in touch. I was concerned when I didn't hear from you. Let me give you a lift.'

'No, really—there's no need.'

'There is every need. You're shivering with cold.'

She blinked, and realised that he was correct: she *was* shivering, and her light coat offered little defence against the winter chill. She was cold and she was tired and her back was hurting. And, what was more, she thought wretchedly, it was entirely his fault that she was cold, tired and pregnant. Why on earth was she trying to conceal her tummy from the man who had got her into this condition?

In a sudden movement that took him by surprise she stepped past him and clambered into the limousine. The warmth and comfort of the opulent vehicle felt like a cocoon to her weary bones.

'We could dine at my hotel,' Shahir murmured.

'I'd have to go home first…' As Kirsten heard herself virtually agreeing to his invitation, she was disconcerted to appreciate that her tongue seemed to be running ahead of her brain.

Without comment, Shahir asked for her address and passed it to his chauffeur. She watched him from below her lashes the whole time, devouring every aspect of his appearance with a voracious craving for detail. Even the way he sat was graceful, with his proud dark head at an angle, his broad shoulders relaxed back, long lean limbs arranged with careless masculinity. She loved the way he dressed too, with a style that was both elegant and fashionable. His designer suit was perfectly tailored to his powerful physique. He always looked as if he had stepped straight out of a glossy magazine.

He really was incredibly good-looking…sin personified in male flesh, she conceded ruefully. It was little wonder she had fallen stupidly in love and even more stupidly into bed with him.

'I'll only be ten minutes.' Kirsten hurried into the terraced house where she lived.

She lived in a grimy street lined with rundown housing. Shahir had to resist the urge to accompany her. At his nod the bodyguard in the front seat got out and alerted the security team in the car behind. He breathed in slow and deep, his brilliant dark eyes bleak, for he was very much shocked by the change in her appearance. Nothing could steal the haunting loveliness from her flawless face, but her skin was as white as milk and as transparent as glass, while her eyes were hollow and darkly shadowed. She had also become painfully thin. She looked ill.

Kirsten fed Squeak. She knew that she was going to tell Shahir about the baby. Not because it felt like the right thing to do, or because it was silly to feel humiliated by a pregnancy that he had inflicted on her. No, primarily she was going to tell Shahir that she was pregnant because she knew it would ruin his day. There it was—a mean, petty, vengeful and absolutely shameful motive. But that was how she felt at that moment.

All of a sudden she was wondering how many other women he had been with over the past seven months. Had he wined and dined them too? Of course she had just been a lowly cleaner, and while he might have been prepared to take that lowly cleaner to bed he had not been democratic enough to offer to take her out for a meal. Or give her a flower…or, for that matter, even a little magazine! She could not even regard herself as having been a cheap date, because there had not been a date to begin with. That acknowledgement did nothing to raise her sagging self-esteem.

She was convinced that while she had been struggling to survive Shahir had been partying. Household gossip had always implied that he led an astonishingly quiet and boring life at Strathcraig. Didn't drink, didn't smoke, did nothing but work, work and work, what free time he did have absorbed by the charitable foundation he had set up.

Kirsten, however, was unimpressed by that account of clean and decent living. Shahir might not have brought women he slept with to the castle, but he owned other properties round the world, and he had asked her to be his mistress, hadn't he? He had also got her into bed faster than the speed of light, which signified no small amount of experience, she reasoned bitterly. Any man who kept a mistress was a womaniser. He might be a discreet womanizer, but he was a womaniser nonetheless.

Now she had stoked her hatred to new and heady heights, she saw that it was time that he knew exactly what she thought of him!

Squeak had arthritic joints, and had to be lifted into the limousine. Once on board, he curled up in the cosiest corner of the carpeted floor and went straight back to sleep. Kirsten sank heavily into the leather seat opposite Shahir and closed her eyes while she planned the speech she would make to him. Exhaustion weighed her down like a heavy blanket…

The unfamiliar sound of Squeak growling wakened Kirsten from her heavy slumber. Blinking drowsily, she gazed down at Squeak who, having stationed himself protectively in front of her, was baring his teeth at Shahir, leaning forward.

'I was trying to wake you. He is a good watchdog,' Shahir advanced dryly. 'We've arrived at the hotel.'

'Sorry—I must have dozed off.' Running an uneasy hand through her rumpled hair, Kirsten took hold of Squeak's lead. 'Where are we?'

'In the hotel's underground car park. Did you think I was abducting you?'

Kirsten forced a laugh. 'Don't be daft.'

As she walked into the lift, Squeak, agitated by his unfamiliar surroundings, crossed in front of her and she stumbled over his lead. Shahir closed firm hands to her shoulders to steady her before she could tumble forward. 'Careful…'

Without appreciating how close he was to her, Kirsten spun nervously round to face him again. Unfortunately her tummy got in the way of her smoothly completing the movement and rubbed against his hip. She glanced down and was transfixed by the way the fabric of her coat had pulled taut over her projecting midsection to define her fecund shape with cruel accuracy.

Bemused by her tense silence, Shahir followed the path of her gaze. Everything that had confused him fell into place: her ill-health, her unusually clumsy gait, the slowness with which she now moved.

At their feet Squeak growled at the tall dark man's proximity, but he was ignored. Shahir lifted hands that were not quite steady and undid the two buttons on her coat and carefully spread the edges apart. 'You're going to have a baby,' he breathed, his entire focus pinned to the sizeable swell of her belly. 'And soon. Whose baby?'

Kirsten dug her hands into her pockets and used them to whip shut the coat and conceal her stomach again. Her face was as red as fire. 'Whose do you think?' she hissed like a stinging wasp, accusation etched in every syllable.

'Then the baby will be due within the next few weeks…'

'I'm glad you can count,' she commented thinly.

A servant already had the door of his penthouse suite open in readiness.

Shahir felt light-headed. If his calculations were correct, in less than two months he would be a father. He was in shock. So he was not to feature as a statistic in the much-discussed global fall in male fertility. The baby she was carrying was his. Of course it was. Did that explain why she looked so ill? He knew less than nothing about pregnant women. But what he did know sent a cold shiver through him, for his own mother had died bringing him into the world.

Kirsten came to a self-conscious halt in the centre of the luxurious sitting room. 'I want you to know that I hate you for getting me into this situation,' she told him with feverish force. 'I really, really hate you for it!'

Shahir released his breath in a soundless hiss. She was understandably upset, he reasoned. She must have had a rough time in recent months, and she was clearly unwell. But now that he was here to take care of her everything was about to change. The world would literally become her oyster.

He was tempted to scoop her into his arms and race for the airport at speed, but he knew he couldn't take her back to his own country to enjoy the very best of tender care until she was his wife.

'Did you hear me?' Kirsten demanded, a tad shrilly.

'Yes. I acknowledge that we have not enjoyed a conventional relationship—'

'We didn't have a relationship…you slept with me!'

'Dragging up the past in an emotional way at this point is not constructive. You are expecting my child, and that is the key issue at stake here. It is vitally important that we marry as soon as it can be arranged,' Shahir declared without hesitation, lean, powerful features taut. 'Why? Because our baby will be heir to the throne of Dhemen—but *only* if his birth is legitimate.'

Unprepared for either of those two announcements, Kirsten stared back at him in a daze of angry confusion. 'You still haven't said anything about what I said.'

'Right now I would be grateful if you would acknowledge that we currently have a much more pressing duty towards the child you carry.'

'You're still prepared to marry me?' Without warning her mind had circled back to centre on Shahir's earlier proposition, and there her mind stuck—as though her thoughts were lodged in cement. Once again she was getting the chance to marry Shahir. Pride and a strong sense of fairness had made her refuse his first proposal seven months earlier. She had not needed a wedding ring to compensate her for the loss of her virginity. Even loving him, she hadn't wanted him on those humiliating terms.

'Of course I am. '

'Wouldn't it have been simpler just to take precautions and make sure that this didn't happen in the first place?'

'It would have been. But I didn't.' His strong jawline squared. 'I assure you that I have never before been so careless.'

Although the subject embarrassed her, Kirsten was still amazed that a male of his sophistication and experience should have been so careless as to totally disregard the threat of consequences. 'Didn't it occur to you that you might make me pregnant?'

The faintest hint of colour scored his superb cheekbones. 'By the time I appreciated what I had done, it was too late. Afterwards I confess that I underestimated the level of risk. And although I asked you to stay in contact with me, I didn't seriously consider the likelihood of you having conceived.'

'So how do you feel about it now you do know? Cursed? Bitter? Furious?' Kirsten queried, desperate to get a real live human reaction out of him. She was convinced that he had to be feeling such emotions, even if he was determined not to show them.

'I feel that this is our fate and we must accept it with grace,' Shahir countered with rock-solid assurance.

Her teeth gritted at that suave reply. 'You mentioned something about the baby being the heir to...to a throne? What was that about?'

'I am the Crown Prince of my country. My father, Hafiz, is King of Dhemen.' He awarded her a questioning appraisal. 'Surely that cannot be news to you?'

Kirsten was stunned. She had assumed that the royal family he belonged to was a large one, and that he was only one of a whole bunch of princes. She had not been aware that he was the son of a king—or the next in the royal line of succession. In her brief time working at the castle she had not heard anyone mention those facts.

'Let us eat now...'

A door had been quietly opened into an adjoining room and a beautifully laid table awaited them. She sat down, accepted a glass of water, and sipped at it.

'So, Kirsten. Will you set aside your hostility and agree to become my wife?' Shahir prompted gravely.

'I can't believe that you're prepared to marry a thief,' Kirsten heard herself whisper with malicious intent, and she was shocked at herself.

Challenging dark golden eyes flared and met hers in a head-on collision. 'Life is full of surprises.'

Her face flamed, for she had dimly expected him to

backtrack on that issue. 'I didn't steal that pendant...I'm not a thief.'

Shahir said nothing. He watched her shred her roll and leave it untouched.

Kirsten knew that his silence was as good as a statement of his disbelief, and she had to swallow back a hotheaded further comment. Why was it that whenever she tried to score a point with him she ended up sounding wretchedly childish and provocative? She wanted to argue her innocence, but sensed that it would be a waste of what little energy she had left. Right now, his entire focus was on the child she carried.

He wanted to marry her so that the baby would be born within wedlock. She had to be fair to him. The level of his commitment towards their unborn child was impressive, and the speed with which he had accepted responsibility equally so, she acknowledged unhappily. Of course he didn't care about her personally, but what else could she expect? He wasn't even concerned by the reality that she had sworn undying hatred for him. Evidently he was able to rise above such petty personal feelings and concentrate solely on the baby's needs. Shouldn't she be capable of acting with equal unselfishness?

Unfortunately her private emotions did not feel petty. She had fallen madly in love with Shahir bin Harith al-Assad, and he had hurt her terribly. And she only had to look across the table and notice the spectacular bronze of his eyes to be afraid that she was on the brink of being really badly hurt all over again. But she felt horribly guilty for thinking about herself when his example made it clear that she ought only to be considering what was best for the baby.

'So...will you marry me?' Shahir asked again.

'Yes.' Shadowed green eyes screened, Kirsten shrugged her thin shoulders, as if to suggest that she really couldn't care either way. But she doubted that he was taken in by her play of indifference. In the community in which she had been raised the moral rules were narrow and unforgiving, and to have a baby outside the bonds of matrimony could not feel like anything other than a source of shame to her. It was hugely important to her that her child should not suffer the stigma of illegitimacy, and that he or she should have both a father and a father's name.

'I promise that I will not give you cause to regret the decision. I'll make immediate arrangements for our wedding.' The merest hint of a smile tugging at the edges of his sculpted mouth, Shahir stretched a lean brown hand gracefully across the table to engulf hers.

Pale face tensing, Kirsten snaked her fingers hastily back from that threatened contact. 'Let's not be fake,' she said defensively, pushing the soup plate aside after only one spoonful had passed her lips. 'It's not as though it'll be a proper marriage. It'll only be a pretend one, so that we can put on a respectable front.'

Once again Shahir exercised restraint and said nothing. It might have surprised her, but he was renowned as the diplomat of the royal family. Negotiation was an art at his clever fingertips, and one in which he had great skill. Yet around her he was conscious of being as tactless as an elephant running amok in hobnail boots.

He had yet to work out why all judgement and discretion should desert him with such disastrous effect in her radius, so he embraced silence instead.

CHAPTER SEVEN

'I LOOK like a blob with matchstick arms and legs attached.' Strained green eyes full of disappointment, Kirsten turned away from the reflection taunting her in the mirror. She stiffened as a tiny pain curled in her pelvis, but it faded so fast that she thought it nothing to worry about.

Jeanie planted her hands on her ample hips and dealt the younger woman a reproachful appraisal. 'That's a lovely dress, and you look bonny in it!'

'But I'm huge…' Feeling forlorn, and as unlike a bride as it was possible to feel, Kirsten bent down awkwardly to close her suitcase.

She knew she was being unreasonable. She was heavily pregnant, and not even the most cleverly designed outfit could be expected to conceal that reality. Her suit was cream and trimmed with a coffee fringe that was young and stylish, but it was still maternity wear. Just for the space of that morning she would have given virtually anything to look more like a bride than an expectant mother.

A week had passed since she had accepted Shahir's proposal. In the space of that time she had surrendered her job and her bedsit in exchange for a gold credit card, which she had barely used, two bodyguards and a hotel suite. Squeak had taken to a life of luxury with extraordinary ease. Indeed, the little dog trotted about his newly spacious surroundings with a decided hint of cheerful pomposity, but Kirsten still felt as if she was playing a starring role in someone else's drama.

Shahir had applied for a special licence to enable their wedding to take place quickly, and then he had immediately flown home to Dhemen in order to gain his father's consent to the marriage. He had also insisted that she invite Jeanie down for the wedding. He had phoned her every single day too, she reminded herself dully. He was courteous and considerate and…impersonal. He'd asked her how she felt, but not how she thought, and when she had tried to ask him how his father had reacted to his son and heir's desire to marry a very pregnant foreigner, he had smoothly changed the subject. She didn't blame him for doing so, for on reflection she decided that her question had been an incredibly stupid one. After all, there was no earthly way that King Hafiz of Dhemen could possibly be persuaded to look on her as an acceptable bride for his royal son and heir.

'I have something to tell you that will cheer you up,' Jeanie told her with a grin. 'Would you like to guess what the hottest gossip at the castle was when I left yesterday?'

Kirsten shook her head.

'Everyone reckons that Pamela Anstruther framed you as a thief because she realised that Prince Shahir had fallen madly in love with you!'

Kirsten screened her eyes to conceal her pain. On her wedding day of all days she was all too conscious of the fact that her bridegroom did not love her. At the same time, however, she was extremely relieved to hear that the castle staff had started to question and doubt her guilt.

'Is that really what people think?'

'What else could they think? Lady Posh spent two years throwing herself at the Prince, and it didn't matter how short she wore her skirts—she never got to pull him!

She must've been mad with rage and jealousy when she saw the love story of the century happening right under her nose. I mean, you are absolutely besotted with him, aren't you?'

'Yes,' Kirsten mumbled tightly

'Well, it does my heart good to know that all Lady Posh's spite and scheming came to nothing in the end,' Jeanie declared with strong satisfaction.

'How did Morag Stevens react to the news that Shahir and I were getting married?' Kirsten was keen to find out how the assistant housekeeper, whose damning evidence as a witness had convicted her, had behaved.

'When she heard that you were about to become Strathcraig's new mistress she burst into floods of tears and scuttled away,' the redhead shared, with a meaningful roll of her eyes. 'She's scared stiff—that's what she is!'

The phone buzzed. 'The car's waiting for you.' Jeanie grinned. 'Just think—in a couple of hours you'll be a princess.'

Kirsten looked startled. 'Nobody has said anything about that. I honestly don't think it works quite that way—'

'You mean you pulled a prince and you only get to be an ordinary missus?' Wearing an expression of comical disillusionment, Jeanie shook her head as they left the suite. 'What about the baby? Won't it get a title either?'

Kirsten stepped into the lift. 'I really don't know.'

'His family are probably raging that he isn't marrying a royal princess!' Jeanie clamped a guilt-stricken hand to her lips. 'Scratch that—forget I opened my big mouth.'

Kirsten stiffened. 'Why? I bet it's true. Remember how shocked you were when I admitted who the father of my baby was!'

'Yeah…but when I stopped to think about it,' Jeanie answered chirpily, 'Prince Shahir getting off with the most gorgeous good-living virgin under the castle roof is really not that surprising. I mean, there's not a lot else to do at Strathcraig. Now, don't forget that I'm leaving straight after the service at the church with Douglas and Elspeth—'

'Jeanie…that's silly,' Kirsten protested, and not for the first time. 'We're going to a hotel for a meal. Please join us.'

The plump redhead groaned out loud and laughed. 'You won't change my mind about this. No way am I sitting down to eat with a prince…I'd be so nervous I couldn't eat!'

Donald had offered to give Kirsten away at the ceremony, but Kirsten had thanked him and gently refused. It was to be a very quiet wedding, with witnesses only, and she saw no reason to slavishly follow tradition. In fact, she thought that plain and simple suited the nature of the occasion best. It did hurt that she had not a single relative to attend. She would have loved to have had her brother Daniel with her, but she had no idea where he was. After mustering her courage she had phoned her father to tell him that she was getting married, but Angus Ross had put the phone down the minute he had heard his daughter's voice.

She had told herself that such things scarcely mattered. After all, it was to be a marriage of convenience, forged primarily for their baby's benefit. The ring she would receive would not be given with love, or even with respect, she conceded painfully. Shahir still believed that she was a thief, so how could he possibly respect her?

Even so, she had felt that his misconception should not prevent her from recognising their child's right to the legitimate birth that would enable him to be fully accepted by his father's family. But his lack of faith in her still stung like acid. On the other hand the gossip that Jeanie had mentioned made the situation look a good deal brighter. Surely if other people suspected Lady Pamela, and Morag Stevens had lied, Shahir would eventually accept her innocence?

'Go get him, girl!' Jeanie whispered cheekily in Kirsten's ear as she began to move down the aisle of the church.

Her cheeks warming, Kirsten made a covert appraisal of the tall, dark and extravagantly handsome male at the altar. There was a younger man standing by Shahir's side, but she spared the stranger the merest glance because it had been a week since she had last seen Shahir and to her it felt like half a lifetime.

There was no point denying it any longer, she thought ruefully. All that talk about loathing him had just been a brick to hurl for want of any other—a face-saving, juvenile lie. The truth was that she was crazy about him. The sound of his voice on the phone gave her butterflies. When he smiled it was as if wings were attached to her heart.

Spectacular eyes that were the colour of bronze in the dim interior met hers, but he did not smile and she lowered her gaze again.

The service was short. As she made her responses she found that she was very nervous, and she wondered if that was why her skin felt so oddly clammy.

Shahir slid a ring on to her wedding finger and tears flooded her eyes. He was her husband now. She blinked, terrified he would notice her tears and wonder what was the matter with her. Lowering her lashes, however, she hovered lest he wanted to seize the opportunity to kiss her.

'You're as a white as a ghost,' Shahir remarked in a taut undertone, making it evident that kissing could not have been further from his mind.

A single tiny compliment, even a hint of a compliment, would have been sufficient to make the day a happy one for Kirsten. But to be told she resembled the living dead when she had made so much effort to look the very best she could was the equivalent of having a vampire's stake driven through her heart.

'I suppose that is why you look as if you're attending a funeral rather than your own wedding?' his bride whispered back flatly.

'It is a solemn occasion.' His hand closed over hers, his thumb resting against a slender wrist which felt as fragile as the bones of a tiny bird in his careful hold.

Shahir was seriously worried about her health. When he asked her how she was she always said she was fine, but she looked really ill to him. She *had* admitted that nausea spoiled her appetite, and perhaps that was all that was the matter. If he expressed his concern he might worry her, and upset her, and he was reluctant to take that risk. In a few hours they were leaving for Dhemen. There, the need for her to meet her new gynaecologist would ensure that she could enjoy an immediate check-up.

Kirsten was reflecting that he hadn't even thought to give her a bouquet to carry. Suddenly her empty hands seemed to emphasise all that their wedding so conspicuously lacked. Love was the obvious missing component—and she had better get used to that, hadn't she? There was no point hankering after what she could not have.

In the church porch, a lively male voice complained, 'How much longer do I have to wait to meet my sister-in-law?'

Kirsten had been so preoccupied with her own feelings that she had forgotten Shahir's companion at the altar.

'Kirsten…' Shahir fell still. 'This is my younger brother, Raza.'

'Had I met you first, Shahir would be the one acting as best man!' Laughing brown eyes twinkled down at her, and then narrowed with an astonishment he couldn't hide when he registered the unmistakable swell of her stomach. 'But obviously I would have had to meet you quite a long time ago to be in with a chance,' he completed, in a teasing recovery.

Shahir said something in his own language, his demeanour and tone as cold and crushing as ice. Kirsten went red, and then white, and hastily turned away to conceal her discomfiture. He had not even told his brother that she was pregnant. Obviously he was ashamed of her, and of her condition, and she felt cut to the bone. Her back was hurting. As she resisted the urge to massage the spot she felt a dragging pain stir low in her tummy, and a slight gasp escaped her.

'What is it?' Shahir asked instantly.

'Pain,' she framed breathlessly. 'It's really bad!'

His magnificent bone structure set hard below the bronzed skin. He addressed his brother in urgent Arabic and then bent down to lift Kirsten slowly and gently up into his arms. 'You should be lying down.'

'Shahir, I'm scared…the baby!' she sobbed fearfully, and then she bit back any further words—for he scarcely needed to be told that she was afraid that she was having a miscarriage.

It was not a fear Kirsten had had to deal with before.

But it swiftly became a terror that engulfed her in a tidal wave of bitter regret. She had taken the stability of her pregnancy and the health of her unborn child for granted while she complained about the nagging nausea that continually spoiled her appetite. That acknowledgement filled her with guilt and dread. She had hardly dared to appreciate the miracle of conception, or look forward to the birth of her future son or daughter. Her rigid upbringing had inhibited such free thinking. She had been desperately ashamed of being an unmarried mother-to-be, and she had punished herself by refusing to find anything positive in her situation.

Was this, then, to be the price she paid for her blindness? she asked herself in a panic. Was she about to lose her baby?

Her fingers splayed against the taut curve of her stomach. Right from the beginning she had loved the tiny life growing inside her with protective intensity. But she had not allowed herself to visualise a little boy with Shahir's silky black hair and raw energy, or a little girl with a feminine version of his imperious brows and the dazzling gift of his charisma. That would have been a step too far for her—an exercise in self-indulgence that she could not allow herself to enjoy.

Choking back a sob, she squeezed her eyes tight shut and prayed.

Shahir made her lie down full-length in the limousine, and positioned himself by her head. He wound her fingers comfortingly within his. 'We will be at the hospital within five minutes, and the best of care will be yours.'

'I bet you weren't expecting this today,' Kirsten muttered jaggedly.

'Try to keep calm...' Shahir smoothed the hair back from her temples in a soothing gesture. 'When I am with you, you should not be afraid. I will not allow any harm to come to you, and no trouble is so hard to bear when it is shared.'

Kirsten tried to comfort herself with the hope that her pregnancy was far enough advanced for the baby to have a good chance of survival if she went into premature labour. But what if there was something wrong and she was losing their child?

The medical facility she entered was unlike any hospital she had ever visited. The last word in high-tech gleaming luxury, it was a private clinic attached to the charitable foundation that Shahir ran. She was whisked into an examination room at speed. A consultant arrived, and told her that she would have to be admitted and that the following few hours would be crucial.

Helped into bed by a nurse, Kirsten was relieved that the cramping little pains which she had been suffering seemed to be in the process of subsiding.

'You should go and get something to eat,' Kirsten told Shahir, when he entered her private room ten minutes later.

He studied her in polite astonishment. 'Are you joking?'

'There's no reason why you should go hungry.'

'Right now I'm staying here with you.'

'You don't have to,' she told him, but she didn't mean it; just at that moment she did not want to let him out of her sight.

'No matter what, I'll be here.'

That declaration impressed her, and the worst of her tension seeped away. She made herself a little more comfortable in the bed, and a yawn crept up on her out of nowhere. 'I'm so tired…' she whispered apologetically.

'Then try to sleep,' Shahir suggested. 'I'll wake you up if anything happens.'

A drowsy giggle escaped her as she tried to imagine what could happen that she might contrive to sleep through.

She had not actually believed that she would sleep, but she did manage to doze for a while. When her eyes opened fuzzily again the first thing she noticed was her own hand, where it rested on the pillow, and her wedding ring glinting shiny and new on her finger. Shahir was lodged by the window, his back turned to her. Raw tension was etched into the set line of his broad shoulders and the spread of his long powerful legs.

'I bet this isn't how you planned to spend your wedding day...'

Shahir swung round, glittering golden eyes zeroing in on her with an amount of concern that surprised her and made her regret her tart comment. 'If you are well at the end of it, I will have no complaints. You don't look so pale. Any more pains?'

She shook her head slowly. She was finding it a challenge to remove her attention from him. He was incredibly attractive.

A relieved smile curving his handsome mouth, he approached the bed and gazed down at her. 'You are strong, and so is our child.'

'Will I have to stay in here tonight?'

His dark, deepset eyes narrowed, black eyelashes glinting. 'Yes. Would you like something to eat now?'

'No, thanks.'

'I am worried about the amount of weight you have lost, and so is the doctor,' he reminded her gently.

'Feeling sick all the time makes for a very effective diet. Have you eaten yet?'

'I have been so troubled about you that I haven't even felt hungry,' Shahir confided.

Her green eyes clung to his lean strong face and she sighed. 'All right. I get the message. I will try to eat.'

She managed a small meal, and even savoured half of a chocolate mousse before drifting off to sleep again.

Somewhere in the middle of the night she wakened. A shaded lamp shed light into the corner of the room. Shahir was sprawled in a chair by the bed, and she studied him with admiring eyes. A dark shadow of blue-black stubble roughened his jawline and emphasised the beautiful curve of his expressive masculine mouth.

'Why are you still here?' she whispered, amazed that he had not left her to the care of the medical staff.

Angling his proud head back, Shahir rested dark-as-midnight eyes on her, his surprise at the question unconcealed. 'Where else would I be? You're my bride, and this is our wedding night.'

Kirsten was stunned by that response. She had expected him to say something about his duty of care towards her and the child she carried, or to mention the risk of her going into premature labour. 'I'd forgotten that…'

'I hadn't.' He stretched out a hand and enclosed her fingers in his. 'Go back to sleep.'

Even badly in need of a shave he looked quite astoundingly good-looking. 'Yes, boss.'

He laughed softly, sexily. 'I like the sound of that.'

'I should've known you'd take it the wrong way,' she groaned. 'Will you see that Squeak is looked after?'

'Our staff will take care of him.'

'But he'll be lost without me,' Kirsten pointed out anxiously.

'I will personally check that Squeak is OK. How long has he been with you?'

'My mother gave him to me as a puppy, when I was nine years old. He's thirteen now,' she shared.

'A venerable age. Now, stop worrying.'

Over the following five days it slowly sank in on Kirsten that she had no choice other than to be ultra-careful for what remained of her pregnancy.

'When will we be flying out to Dhemen?' she asked Shahir.

'It would be most unwise for us to attempt the journey now. I am resigned to remaining in London until after the birth,' he countered, with a wry shrug of acceptance. 'It is imperative that you rest. Every day that our child stays in your womb makes him or her stronger, though you will find such inactivity frustrating.'

But Kirsten knew that she would only have to live with those limitations for a matter of weeks, and she was willing to do anything that would help her baby to be born safely and in good health. 'Whatever it takes... Will I have to remain here in the clinic?'

His dark golden eyes were grave. 'No. If you promise to be sensible, you can stay in our London apartment. Nurses will be engaged to care for you.'

'I'll be sensible,' she swore.

Thirty-six hours later, Kirsten left the clinic and was installed in the penthouse apartment, where she enjoyed a rapturous reunion with Squeak and met the first of the three nurses engaged to watch over her in shifts.

The apartment was very large indeed, and furnished for slick city living with not an antique or a traditional rug in sight. Kirsten was soon ensconced in an opulent divan in a vast bedroom which enjoyed a spectacular view of the Thames.

Mid-morning, several large lingerie boxes were delivered. The boxes contained a selection of pure silk and lace nightwear in her favourite pastel shades, and a hand-signed gift card from Shahir. Encouraged by the nurse looking after her, she immediately donned a pale green nightdress with a matching jacket, and submitted to having her hair brushed for his promised visit at lunchtime.

'Do you think you will be comfortable here?' Shahir strode in, coolly immaculate in a light grey business suit. 'My family use this as a base when they visit London. Raza stayed here while he was at university, but he has his own apartment now. Perhaps it is time for me to acquire a more private dwelling?'

As Shahir moved deeper into the room the nurse slipped out, with a coy smile that only embarrassed Kirsten.

'That nurse is acting like we're honeymooners, desperate to be alone with each other,' she muttered apologetically.

In answer, Shahir bent down. Closing one deft hand into the shining fall of her silvery blonde hair, he circled her luscious pink mouth with his until her lips parted and allowed him to delve deep in an expert and provocative foray. Wildly disconcerted by that sensual exploration, Kirsten felt her body quicken with startling urgency. The rosy tips of her breasts pinched tight into a distended and tender fullness that made her whimper low in her throat in disconcertion. Coming down beside her on the bed, Shahir tasted her lips slowly and hungrily, and then lifted his dark head.

'If only we were free to take advantage of being alone…but we're not. The sweetest pleasures are always forbidden.' A wicked smile slashed his lean, savagely handsome features with a wildness that shocked her as much as it excited her. 'But the knowledge that you desire me as much as I desire you helps me to be patient.'

Ludicrously unprepared for his confrontation, which had come out of nowhere at her, Kirsten quivered with outrage and uncertainty. 'But that's not true!'

Assured brown fingers smoothed over the prominent thrust of her pouting breasts beneath the fine silk, teasing at the stiff and straining crests she would have hidden from him had she only had the opportunity. With a moan of shame she flushed to the roots of her hair and shut her eyes tight, even though she was guiltily conscious that she was revelling in the achingly sweet tingling of her sensitive flesh.

'Your body knows me—and the truth. Were it possible I would lie with you now and give you all the pleasure and excitement that you could handle,' Shahir murmured huskily. 'But the present need for restraint will make those delights all the more intense when the time comes.'

'This is supposed to be a fake marriage!' Kirsten framed in shaken protest.

'That was your idea. Is it also your wish? What benefit would such an arrangement offer to either of us? I don't do fake,' Shahir enumerated with precision. 'You are my wife, whom I would protect with my life, and soon you will be the mother of my child. I want nothing false or pretend in our marriage. Did I mention that there will be a second wedding held for us in Dhemen?'

She stared back at him, her eyes clinging to his lean strong face, to the fierce resolve etched there. 'No...you didn't.'

'Perhaps by then you too will know what you want. Even were we able to share a bed now I would prefer to honour you by restraining my ardour until you are considered truly mine by all my family,' he admitted levelly.

'Will your family accept me?' she asked in sudden apprehension.

'Of course,' he said gently. 'For the sake of appearances a polite fiction has been coined. According to that story, we married in secret last year because my father disapproved of our match and withheld his consent for an official wedding. The imminent birth of our child can in that way be viewed as having softened the King's heart into accepting the wife I chose for myself, and nobody loses face.'

Kirsten veiled her eyes, for she was thinking that he had *not* chosen her. Sexual attraction had overruled self-discipline, and the price of succumbing to temptation had been high. But possibly he had paid the highest price, because he did not love her as she loved him and she would never be the wife he would have chosen for himself.

'That soft shade of green suits you to perfection,' he remarked huskily. 'Your hair looks like white-gold against it.'

'I didn't even say thank you for your gifts... Thank you—you picked beautiful things.'

'It was nothing. I only suggested the colours.' Honesty bade him admit it, and a faint darkening of colour emphasised the stunning angle of his proud cheekbones. 'I was lost when it came to styles, although I mentioned what I thought you would like to the manageress.'

Kirsten was watching him in fascination. 'Haven't you bought anything like this before?'

He frowned at the idea. 'No...but if I didn't take care of it, who else was there to do it?'

Kirsten dropped her head to conceal the smile creeping

over her lips. Evidently he had made a special effort on her behalf, and shopping for such intimate apparel had rather embarrassed him. She was delighted to discover that she was the very first woman he had bought lingerie for. Maybe he wasn't quite as much of a womaniser as she had imagined…

'Ah!' she gasped abruptly, pressing her palm to the side of her tummy as the baby chose that instant to kick with vigour.

'The baby?' His spectacular golden eyes shimmered and he moved closer and extended a lean, bronzed hand. 'May I?'

Her hesitation was brief. 'Yes…'

He spread gentle fingers to the firm swell of her belly and laughed out loud with satisfaction. His wonder and pride were reflected in his eloquent gaze. 'What joy you are bringing me,' he murmured, with a sincerity that touched her deep.

Shahir might not love her, but on the other hand he certainly didn't seem to feel trapped by her pregnancy, she reflected with satisfaction. His genuine pleasure at the prospect of fatherhood meant a great deal to her. He definitely wanted their unborn child, and was prepared to celebrate his or her arrival rather than simply accept it as an inevitable event. Furthermore, although she currently had as much shape as a barrel and could not see her feet, remarkably Shahir still seemed to find her attractive. Those were very strong positives to build on, Kirsten told herself dizzily.

Yet for all that she was married to a man who still firmly believed she was a thief.

That unwelcome recollection hit her like a bucket of icy water. With difficulty she suppressed her hurt and resentment on that score. Although it mortified her to acknowledge the fact, she felt that Shahir had barely known her as a person before he had swept her into bed at Strathcraig, and he had misjudged her accordingly. Now they were finally getting to know each other, and forming a real relationship with bonds that were new and fragile. And she did not want to damage those bonds by staging a confrontation too soon. After all, what evidence of her innocence could she offer him? She had none. But when Shahir had a better understanding of her she would reopen the subject of her supposed dishonesty, and insist that he hear her out with a more open mind, she decided tautly.

The next morning she was having breakfast when a sizeable bundle of magazines and books arrived. She smiled at yet another demonstration of his thoughtfulness. Without thinking about nausea or appetite, or indeed noticing the presence or lack of either, she somehow managed to happily work her way through a bowl of cereal, a whole buttered croissant and two cups of hot chocolate.

Over the couple of weeks that followed Shahir spent all of his free time with her, but even though she would not have objected he did not make any attempt to kiss her again.

Like Squeak, she found herself yawning and nodding off to sleep with very little warning.

Shahir cancelled his business trips abroad, and tried not to travel too far out of reach, and as her due date drew closer she felt more secure when he was around. The consultant had already warned her that the baby was too large for her narrow pelvis and would have to be delivered by Caesarean section.

In the end, she went into labour a fortnight early. It was mid-morning, and Shahir was on the other side of

London. She had already been admitted to the clinic when he arrived there.

'You will be absolutely fine…you will feel no pain,' he whispered urgently, holding her hand a little too tightly for comfort. 'I have discussed it fully with the surgical team. There is to be no pain…not even a twinge. I could not bear to see you suffer.'

Below his bronzed skin he was pale as death and tense as a steel girder. He seemed much more afraid for her than she was for herself. She was already suffering slight contractions, and she did not think it was possible to give birth without enduring some level of discomfort, but evidently nobody had dared to tell him that. Worried that even a moan from her might utterly unnerve him, she embraced a stoic silence until the medication kicked in.

Shahir was struggling not to betray his fear for her, and he was praying. He knew his own family history too well to assume that nothing would go wrong. Even the best medical attention could not guarantee a happy conclusion to every birth. His own mother had been young and healthy, but she had died soon after his birth from a seizure. His father had never really recovered from the loss of the wife he had adored.

Within half an hour their little boy was delivered, with an amazing lack of fuss.

Shahir touched a reverent fingertip to their son's tiny starfish hand and swallowed convulsively, the fierce tension he had endured slowly dissipating.

'He is…he is truly precious,' he breathed thickly, his dark golden gaze shimmering with emotion. 'We are blessed indeed. In a few weeks, when you are well enough to travel, we will take him home to Dhemen and show him to my people.'

CHAPTER EIGHT

WHEN the jet landed in Dhemen, Kirsten lifted her son Tazeem out of his travelling bassinet the instant she was free to undo her seat belt. Cradling his warm little body with tender care, she dropped a kiss on his satin-smooth cheek.

'Who is the most beautiful little boy in the world?' she whispered.

Tazeem opened big dark brown eyes that promised to be a mirror match of his handsome father's and studied her with the unflinching regard that was equally reminiscent of his genes. He was a good-natured baby, but he had a strong will as well and could complain bitterly if given cause. She smiled down at him, noting the warm colour in his cheeks and the clearness of his eyes with satisfaction.

For the first few weeks after his premature birth, Tazeem had demonstrated a dismaying tendency to pick up every stray infection going. Shahir and Kirsten had begun to worry that their child's early arrival in the world had undermined his health. When the little boy overcame those initial setbacks and went from strength to strength his parents had been hugely relieved. Even so, their natural disquiet had disrupted their plans to travel.

Kirsten had ended up staying with Tazeem in London while Shahir flew round the world dealing with all the business concerns that had had to take a back seat while Kirsten was unwell. Tazeem was now seven weeks old, and it was three weeks since Kirsten had seen his father.

As a result of what felt like very serious deprivation, Kirsten's eyes were sparkling with anticipation. She could hardly wait to see Shahir again. He had been wonderfully kind and supportive after Tazeem's birth, especially as it had taken time for her to recover from surgery. And having said that he would honour her by not consummating their marriage until after their second wedding had taken place, he had adhered so rigidly to that decision that he had not even kissed her.

In truth it had been hard for Kirsten not to feel rejected, and even harder for her to overcome the suspicion that Shahir was not unduly taxed by his restraint because he no longer found her much of a temptation. Indeed, it seemed to her that she was continually faced with the humiliating reality that a shotgun wedding such as theirs carried no promise of love or even desire—only the far more prosaic assurance that their child's needs had taken precedence over their own.

Passing her infant son over to the caring attentions of his nurse, Kirsten rose with a rueful sigh from her comfortable seat and prepared to leave the jet. Long before landing she had taken the chance to freshen up, and had changed into the blue suit she had picked with care for her arrival in the kingdom of Dhemen. She had read every book about her husband's country that she could lay her hands on. Certain colours were considered auspicious, and blue was one of them.

Hearing Shahir's rich dark drawl, she realised that the cabin door was already open and that her husband must have come to collect her off the jet. Delighted by what she assumed to be his impatience to see her, she hurried down the aisle to greet him. 'Shahir…'

Brilliant dark as ebony eyes assailed hers and he smiled, his sculpted mouth curving with megawatt charm.

Her heart went on a rollercoaster ride. 'You have been missed,' he murmured, clasping her hand in greeting and then stepping back from her again with a formality that took her by surprise.

'Tazeem…' Shahir paused to look down at his son and laughed softly, 'He looks happy—and so he should be now that he is finally coming home.'

Feeling rather hurt by his cool, calm welcome, Kirsten bent to glance out of the nearest window. She was aghast when she saw the serried ranks of people standing out in the baking sun. 'Oh, my goodness, what's going on? Who are they waiting for?'

'You and Tazeem. Are you ready? It would be most discourteous to keep our well-wishers hanging around in this heat.'

'Waiting for me and Tazeem?' Dismay made her voice strike a shrill note. 'My goodness…'

'All you have to do is smile. You're a bride, and already the mother of the second in line to the throne. You are also incredibly beautiful. All of those facts will ensure that you are very popular,' Shahir pointed out bracingly, while he edged her with gentle determination towards the exit.

The sunlight almost blinded her and the heat closed round her like a velvet cocoon. A band struck up a rousing musical arrangement. Before she could carry on down the steps, Shahir closed a staying hand round hers.

'Don't move. Keep your head up,' he instructed, half under his breath. 'That's our national anthem.'

Embarrassed pink suffused her fine skin.

At the foot of the steps a few minutes later, Shahir exchanged salutes with a man in a military uniform. The crowds behind the barriers bowed and cheered and applauded, but did so in a very restrained and respectful way. Shahir guided her straight into the welcome shade of an elaborate marquee, where she was ushered towards the seats raised on a dais.

'Don't sit down until I do,' Shahir warned her in an undertone, belatedly appreciating that she would have to be taught royal protocol—and fast.

It was dawning on him that he had been thoughtless in not equipping her better for the challenge of this rarefied world in which he lived. The many privileges of royal status came at the cost of an equal number of restrictions. When his wife appeared in public she would be expected to demonstrate an impeccable grasp of etiquette and the old-fashioned formality that was the hallmark of his family.

An adorable little girl presented Kirsten with a beautiful bouquet of flowers. Kirsten's generous smile lit up her face and she thanked the child in Arabic, grateful that she had taken the time to learn a few basic words.

'I'm impressed,' Shahir admitted.

'Don't be,' she said shyly. 'I bought a tourist vocabulary book and I've only managed to learn about fifty words.'

A court ministerial advisor gave a rather lengthy speech of welcome with great enthusiasm. Then an impossibly long white limousine with a Dhemeni flag on the bonnet pulled up, and at Shahir's covert signal they stood up and left the dais. The band immediately began to play a classical piece that was familiar to her.

'In your honour, the musicians have selected a piece by an English composer,' Shahir explained.

She was touched. 'It's called "Chanson de Matin." It was a favourite of my mother's.'

For an instant he was surprised, until he recalled that

her mother had taught music. 'I didn't realise you were so knowledgeable.'

'I was still quite young when my father decided to get rid of the family television. Mum used music to keep Daniel and I occupied in the evenings. We were quite happy without a TV. Then Dad decided we were enjoying music too much and he sold the piano.'

His fine ebony brows pleated. 'It must have been grim.'

'It hurt Mum the most, and I promised myself that one day I would have a piano of my own and I would play it all day!' Kirsten confided with a rueful laugh. 'I'd be pretty rusty at the keyboard now.'

His dark golden eyes had a sombre light. 'I don't think that would matter.'

The interior of the air-conditioned limo was blissfully cool, and Kirsten stretched out her long slender legs and relaxed with a contented little sigh.

Shahir studied her delicate profile with keen masculine appreciation. Her wilful independent streak was matched by a surprising level of sensitivity. The more he found out about her, the more he wanted to know. Like an exquisite painting, she never lost her appeal. And the plain tailored suit she wore was the perfect choice for a woman of such stunning beauty. In so many ways, he acknowledged, she continually exceeded his expectations.

But no sooner had that thought occurred to him than he remembered the theft of the pendant. His proud bone structure hardened, and distaste filled him before he could suppress it. He removed his attention from her. Once again he reminded himself that she had made an appalling mistake in fraught circumstances, and that he had to find it within himself to understand and forgive.

'My word!' Kirsten sat bolt upright, her eyes rounding

in astonishment when she saw the giant advertising hoarding on the outskirts of the city. Unbelievable as it seemed to her, it carried a huge picture of her face and Shahir's. 'I don't believe what I'm seeing. What's that for?'

'It is announcing our wedding, which will be a public holiday. All of Dhemen will be celebrating with us,' Shahir proffered coolly.

She swallowed hard and wondered why he was being so distant with her. Was he wishing he did not have to go through another wedding with her? Was it the ultimate horror to be forced to marry the wrong woman twice over? Or was she simply being over-sensitive? It was not his fault that she suffered from such low self-esteem, she told herself uncomfortably.

The capital city, Jabil, was composed of wide thoroughfares shaded by mature trees. The busy streets were softened by enticing glimpses of lush green parks. Contemporary buildings sat side by side with ancient domed mosques and rambling villas, and there was a definite air of prosperity to the upmarket shops and hotels. The people wore both European and Arab dress, and many of them stopped to look and wave as the royal motorcade rolled past complete with outriders on motorcycles.

'We are to have a traditional wedding,' Shahir breathed tautly, suspecting that culture shock was about to engulf his European bride. 'The festivities begin tonight and will not end until late tomorrow. We will not meet again until the ceremony takes place.'

Kirsten was thoroughly dismayed at the prospect of being parted from him again so soon. 'Does it have to be like that? I mean, why can't we be together?'

The note of panic in her soft voice tugged at his self-assurance until it broke through his defensive barriers. Dark golden eyes intent on her, he closed a lean bronzed hand over hers. 'It is the way it has been done for centuries, and we have broken quite enough rules already in our courtship. As it is, the usual three days of festivities are being compressed into one and a half to suit my father's schedule.'

'But I don't know anybody...' She could hear her voice wobbling and she was ashamed of the tears gathering.

Shahir reached for her other hand as well. 'But there are many English speakers in my family, and they will be very kind to you,' he swore. 'My relatives are very relieved that I have finally found myself a wife.'

The level of his conviction soothed her. 'Relieved?' she queried.

'Apparently my father didn't put any pressure on me to marry because he believed that was the best way to encourage me to take a bride.' His darkly handsome features were wry. 'But I was in no hurry, and my indifference had become a source of concern.'

Curiosity about Faria stabbed at her. How many people were aware that he loved another woman? Had the awareness that his son could not have the woman he really wanted lain behind his royal parent's willingness to be patient?

'Why was the King so worried?'

Amusement gleamed in his stunning eyes. 'As you will learn, my father is a great pessimist. He thought that even after I married it might take years for me to father a child. He even considered the idea that I or my bride might prove incapable of that feat. It is safe to say that he looked at every negative possibility to such an extent that you and Tazeem together make a really winning package.'

She stretched her lips into a forced smile and hid the fact that once again she felt hurt and mortified. Naturally the need and ability to provide a royal son and heir was hugely important in a feudal kingdom with a hereditary line of rulership. Shahir was only being honest about the fact that as far as his father was concerned her greatest gift was her proven aptitude in the fertility stakes. Certainly it was true that she had fallen pregnant easily.

My goodness—had he told his father just *how* easily? Inwardly she absolutely cringed.

'How much did you tell your father about how we met and…er…stuff?'

'I told him the truth.'

Kirsten tensed in consternation. 'So you told him… What did you tell him?'

His imperious black brows pleated as though he considered that a strange question. 'That I had seduced a virgin…what else?'

'But that information wasn't for sharing!' Kirsten launched at him aghast, her face hot as fire. 'That was between us, and private.'

'Not in this case.' His lean strong face betrayed not a trace of regret. 'For your sake I needed to be sure that my father put any blame he wished to bestow on my shoulders, where it belonged. And he did.'

Kirsten breathed in deep and tried to master her embarrassment.

The motorcade was already moving swiftly along the highway that led out of the city. Ahead lay the Ahmet Palace, the private home of the Dhemeni royal family since the seventh century. High fortress walls studded with towers surrounded the vast complex which was spread across a hill. That much alone the books had told her, but no further details had been given. On either side of the road stretched a rolling landscape of sand dunes that disappeared into the distance—terracotta in colour on the shaded side, glistening gold in the harsh sunlight of late afternoon.

They passed through a vast medieval gateway, but even as her curious eyes were widening to absorb the great domed entrance of the nearest building, and the red carpet awaiting their arrival, another daunting thought was occurring to her.

'You didn't tell your father about the theft thing, did you?'

Beneath her scrutiny, Shahir froze to carved ice. 'I presume you are joking? My father believes you to be a woman of irreproachable good character and virtue.'

Anger and pain coalesced inside Kirsten and flared up in a spirited venting of all her pent-up emotions. Green eyes bright as the heart of a fire, she rounded on him. 'Shahir, I've kept quiet about this for far too long, and I think I've been really stupid. I thought that as you got to know me you might start doubting my guilt without me having to plead my own case. For goodness' sake, don't you know anything about me yet? I did not steal that pendant—nor did I put greedy hands on that woman's stupid brooch! Isn't it about time that you accepted that I'm telling you the truth?'

'Please don't shout at me!' Shahir grated.

'Maybe I'm shouting because you're as stubborn as a rock and you just make up your mind about things and won't listen to any other version!' she condemned heatedly. 'But this is my reputation we're talking about, and I've never stolen anything in my life.'

'This is not the time for this, and I do not respond to the aggressive approach.'

'Well, I'm not being humble about it!' Kirsten informed him in a fiery interruption. 'The rumour at Strathcraig is that Lady Pamela set me up because she saw that you were attracted to me. Unfortunately I don't have the slightest idea why the witness lied and said she saw me put the pendant in my locker. But the point is you're my husband. Instead of hammering on about how honourable you are, and how you would protect me with your life, you should get out there and *prove* that I can depend on you—clear my name!'

Shahir was livid with a dark fury as volatile as volcanic lava. How dared she question his honour? How dared she scorn his protection? And as for the theft—how could she possibly believe that he wanted to accept that she was a thief? But the case against her was watertight and left no room for doubt. Had it been otherwise he would have moved heaven and earth to clear her name.

Yet for the first time he was being presented with the possibility that there might have been a deliberate conspiracy aimed at discrediting Kirsten. That risk had not occurred to him. How likely was it, though? He had suspected that Pamela Anstruther had noticed that he had a degree of interest in Kirsten. Could the other woman have come to view Kirsten as a rival and set out to plot her downfall?

Even furious as he was, Shahir knew he would have to check out that angle. But surely it was a fanciful idea?

The passenger door beside him sprang open. He stepped out of the limo. The Court Chamberlain bowed low. Tazeem was borne out of the limousine behind with reverent hands and extended to his father with great care.

Recognising the solemnity of the occasion, Shahir accepted his infant son and waited for Kirsten to emerge.

Kirsten was trembling. Words had exploded from her like uncontrolled missiles and she was in shock in the aftermath of that complete loss of temper. She had suppressed her feelings about the theft for too long because she had been afraid to reopen the subject with Shahir. Unfortunately all that hurt and resentment had broken through at a moment when her nerves were already on edge.

A slim brunette in her late twenties, with gentle dark eyes and creamy skin, moved forward. A long line of servants were bowing their heads at their approach.

Shahir murmured, 'My sister, Jahan…'

Jahan greeted her with a warm smile. 'You are very welcome to your new home. We are all very excited to be celebrating a wedding in the family again.'

A cluster of people eager to see Tazeem now surrounded Shahir.

'My brother will take your son to meet His Majesty the King. You will meet our father at the wedding,' Jahan imparted. 'Will you come this way now?'

Still shaken up after the blistering verbal attack she had launched on Shahir, Kirsten glanced anxiously in her royal husband's direction. For a split second he met her gaze in a head-on collision as physically disturbing as a crash. Her heartbeat jumped and her tummy muscles clenched tight with nerves. His lean, darkly handsome features were as impassive as ever, but she knew as surely as if he had spoken that cold anger still divided him from her with the efficacy of a solid sheet of ice.

At that moment she would have given just about anything to get just five minutes alone with him. Having waited too long to broach the thorny topic of her supposed dishonesty, she had gone overboard and attacked when she should have reasoned and explained. With a sinking heart she realised that in her distress she had been downright offensive. But unhappily, Jahan was urging her to follow her, and there was no way that Kirsten could have any private speech with Shahir.

'This evening you are to have a surprise,' Jahan announced with satisfaction as they crossed a huge echoing stone hall floored with worn marble and entered a passage that appeared to lead into a more modern part of the palace. 'A happy surprise, I hope. Shahir has been very busy on your behalf.'

Kirsten had no idea what Shahir's sister was talking about. Although she kept a polite smile of interest on her face she was still too upset by the argument she had had with Shahir to concentrate. 'A surprise?'

'To tell you about it would spoil it.' Jahan paused outside a door. 'Would you like to wait in here for Tazeem to be brought back to you?'

Surprised that she was being left to her own devices, Kirsten opened the door. 'Will he be long?'

'Half an hour at most....'

Jahan seemed to be waiting for something to happen. Her brow indenting, Kirsten entered the room, and then came to a surprised halt when she saw the tall broad male standing by the window. His hair was the same unusual shade of pale blond as her own. He too looked anxious. Her throat tightened and she stared, almost afraid to credit the powerful sense of recognition she was experiencing, for his features had been familiar to her from childhood on.

'Daniel...?' she whispered uncertainly, for when her brother had left home he had been a painfully thin teenager and this was a man.

'Yeah…it's me.' Her brother's voice was gruff with restrained emotion.

It was the telling glimmer of moisture in his eyes that convinced her that he was real, and she raced across the room and flung herself at him with a sob of happiness and welcome.

CHAPTER NINE

IT WAS some time before either Kirsten or Daniel paused long enough between questions to draw breath. After all, brother and sister had five years of news to catch up on. But, first and foremost, Kirsten could not be persuaded to talk about her own life until Daniel had explained how Shahir had managed to trace him.

'I haven't yet met your husband, but we've talked on the phone. Shahir hired investigators to go and ask questions of just about everybody who ever knew me. That helped to build up a profile of me, and one of my school-teachers mentioned that at one stage I'd been hoping to go to university to do marine biology—'

'Until Dad said you had to work on the farm,' Kirsten recalled heavily.

'Maybe he was right about me just wanting to be a lazy student,' Daniel teased. 'I'm studying for a doctorate now. The detective agency found me by checking out the universities. I've been working abroad on a research project, so they only caught up with me the day before yesterday, and this is as soon as I could get here.'

Slowly Kristin shook her head, fighting back tears. 'I just can't quite believe you *are* here.'

He compressed his mouth ruefully. 'I should have come home to see that you were OK a long time ago.'

'Dad wouldn't have let you into the house.'

'He wouldn't even let me speak to you on the phone, so I gave up ringing.'

'I didn't know you'd phoned,' Kirsten muttered with a painful sense of loss. 'I wish I had.'

'I heard about Mum's death a year after it happened through an old school mate,' he confided heavily. 'I just couldn't handle the fact that I would never see her again because I hadn't been man enough to confront Dad. I felt so guilty.'

'No…you mustn't feel that way. Mum missed you, but she wanted you to have a life of your own. If you had got into a real fight with Dad it would have destroyed her.'

Daniel nodded, too choked up by grief for his late mother to respond.

It was at that point that a knock on the door heralded Tazeem's return. Now enjoying the well-sprung comfort of a magnificent pram wheeled by an English nanny accompanied by two nurses, Tazeem was fast asleep and amusingly unconcerned by the amount of attention he was receiving.

Talk of the promise of the future took over from the hurts and disappointments that Kirsten and Daniel had shared in the past, and Daniel cradled his nephew and grinned. 'I'm actually holding a future king…'

Refreshing mint tea and tiny sweet cakes were brought in and served, and an hour later Kirsten shared an evening meal with her brother in the luxurious suite of rooms allotted for her use. Squeak was waiting there to greet her, and enjoyed a most enthusiastic reunion with his former playmate, Daniel. The little dog would not settle with them, though. He kept on going to the door, sitting down there and sighing heavily.

'What's the matter with him?' her brother asked.

'He's nuts about Shahir,' Kirsten confided with a rueful grin. 'He must know he's around somewhere.'

After the meal, Daniel went off to meet Shahir and join the male wedding party while Kirsten was taken to meet a whole array of Shahir's female relatives. There was one more sister, an array of great-aunts, aunts, and innumerable cousins—and that was not counting those who were related only by marriage to her husband. Tazeem was hugely admired, and Kirsten listened without success for any spoken reference to a woman with the name of Faria.

As she clambered into her comfortable bed at the end of that busy day, her mind was spinning with a myriad of colourful impressions. But all she could actually think about was Shahir, and the reality that there were still hours and hours to be got through before she could see him again. She wondered anxiously if he was still furious with her.

The next day began for her at what felt like the crack of dawn. A delicious breakfast was brought to her in bed, but she had not even finished eating before Jahan came to collect her and escort her to another, older part of the palace.

'The bride receives every possible beauty procedure,' Jahan explained earnestly. 'We want you to relax and enjoy the preparations. It should be a lot of fun.'

The Ahmet Palace was an ancient building like a huge labyrinth. From the outside it resembled a desert fortress, but within the high stone walls it was a complex composed of airy pavilions and tranquil courtyards punctuated with delicate minarets and beautiful gardens. Buildings were linked by stone staircases and roofed walkways.

A little nervous of what might be part and parcel of the bridal preparations, Kirsten watched Tazeem being taken off to the nursery. Maids came to help her undress, and she was so shy at removing her clothes in front of them that they giggled and put up a screen to preserve her modesty. Wrapped in a capacious towel and accompanied by Jahan, she emerged from behind its cover. They entered a great domed and tiled steam room.

'My word...' she sighed, examining her surroundings with wide eyes full of curiosity. 'How old is this place?'

'It was once part of the old harem,' Jahan informed her.

'It's like something out of a film,' Kirsten carolled. 'Jahan...if I wanted to speak to Shahir how would I go about it?'

'You could speak to him on the phone.'

Kirsten nodded at that obvious answer, and wished she had come up with the idea for herself the night before. Working out what she would say, however, was a bigger challenge. How could she ever thank Shahir sufficiently for going to so much trouble to reunite her with her brother? She had not asked him to do that. It had not even crossed her mind that it might be within his power to do that. Yet, without any prompting from her, Shahir had recognised how much it would mean to her to have her brother back in her life.

She sat in the hot, steamy atmosphere mulling over his perception and generosity until a film of perspiration shone on her skin. Two sturdy middle-aged women appeared, divested her of her towel and with great seriousness proceeded to cover her from neck to toe in a substance that resembled green mud.

'It is marvellous for the skin,' Jahan assured her.

Imagining what Shahir would think if he saw her looking like a swamp monster, Kirsten finally started to relax and giggle. When the mud was scrubbed off, she felt as

if her whole body was tingling with cleanliness. In yet
another room her hair was anointed with a herbal preparation, and the palace beautician arrived with her assistant to administer a facial, shape her eyebrows and carry
out a remarkable number of other procedures—all of
which were new to Kirsten's experience.

A buffet lunch was served in a big reception room
furnished with plenty of opulent sofas, and one by one
the other women she had met the evening before began
to filter in. Someone put on some music and the gathering
began to turn into a light-hearted party.

'You must lie down and have a nap now. The bride
has a very long day to get through.' Jahan showed her
into a bedroom overlooking a quiet courtyard.

Kirsten was glad of the privacy, for she had finally
decided what she should say to Shahir. She used the mobile phone he had given her to send him a text that was
just one word long.

Sorry.

The phone was brought to Shahir while he was having a
massage. He read the text and his charismatic smile put
to flight his usual gravity. He didn't text. He might know
how to read them, but he didn't *do* texts. He dismissed
the masseur and rang his wife.

'Kirsten…?'

'I was upset, but I shouldn't have shouted.'

'Your anger had conviction. I will do as you ask. I will
have discreet enquiries made concerning the allegations
that were made against you.' Voicing the decision which
he had reached in the early hours of the morning, Shahir
stretched his long, powerful limbs and shifted into a more
comfortable position on the couch. 'If I have misjudged

you, you are entitled to feel angry. As my wife, it is your right to expect my support.'

Overjoyed that he was finally willing to consider that she might have been framed for the theft at Strathcraig, Kirsten felt a great weight slide off her shoulders. Even so, she could not help saying, 'But I want you to believe in me, Shahir…not just make enquiries because it's your duty to do that like you do everything else.'

Shahir suppressed a groan, for he did not know how to tell her that his whole life was governed by duty—first to the crown of Dhemen and secondly to his family. 'This is our wedding day,' he reminded her. 'I am not thinking of my duty at this moment.'

Kirsten closed her eyes and listened dreamily to the rich dark timbre of his voice. 'What are you thinking of?'

'Lying with you tonight,' he admitted with husky intimacy.

Disconcerted though she was by that candid response, she felt a twist of heat curl low in her pelvis. 'I'm surprised,' she could not resist admitting. 'After all, you're the man who hasn't even kissed me since before Tazeem was born.'

Shahir was startled by that complaint. 'I was showing you respect!'

'Do you still feel *that* guilty about what we did that day at the castle?' Kirsten whispered ruefully, marvelling at how much easier it was to say things on the phone that she would not have dared to say to him face to face.

'No…I think about what we shared far too often,' Shahir confided thickly. 'I remember every second of our passion…'

Her heartbeat accelerated and she blushed. 'That's good.'

'No, it's frustrating. But tonight is my reward for almost a year of cold showers. My reward and your pleasure.'

Her green eyes opened wide. 'Almost a year?' she parroted in astonishment. 'Are you saying—I mean…well, that there hasn't been anyone else?'

'Only you since we first met.'

She squeezed the mobile phone so hard she was vaguely surprised it didn't smash into smithereens. 'I like that. Oh, my goodness—I haven't even thanked you for finding Daniel yet! That was the most wonderful present ever.'

'It was nothing. I have to go,' he told her apologetically. 'My father is waiting.'

Kirsten set aside the phone and stared dizzily into space. Shahir had not made love with anyone since he had swept her off to bed at the castle. Her eyes shone. That thought made her feel very special. Had he desisted from sex out of guilt? She thought about that and decided that in some circumstances guilt was good—especially the kind of guilt that kept Shahir from straying into the beds of other women. For the first time he felt like hers, because he had not touched another woman since first meeting her on the hill above the glen.

When she wakened from her nap she felt as she were in a dream as all the activity of which she was the centre began again, with renewed enthusiasm. Her hair was washed and rinsed until the water ran clear. She bathed in a scented bath and lay down to have perfumed oils rubbed into her skin. While her hair was styled, her nails were manicured, and swirling designs in henna that symbolised good luck and health were skilfully painted on her hands and feet. A make-up artist attended to her face, while her companions chattered and enthused and commented at embarrassing length about how handsome, how virile, how *everything* Shahir was.

When it was time for her to dress, another screen was erected for her with much laughter. She rolled on sheer hold-up stockings edged with lace and donned a long fine silk chemise that felt sensuously soft against her skin. No other lingerie was offered to her. Amazing shoes ornamented with glittering stones were brought for her inspection and slipped on to her feet. Finally she was helped into a fabulously ornate embroidered and beaded robe in royal blue.

'You look amazing.' Jahan drew her out from behind the screen so that all the women could see her, and there was a spontaneous burst of appreciative comment and hand clapping.

Kirsten was transfixed by her unfamiliar reflection in a mirror nearby. She looked incredibly exotic.

She was encouraged to walk round an incense burner three times for good luck.

'The bridal gifts.' Jahan presented her with several boxes. 'We are all eager to see what Shahir has given you.'

'I didn't know there were to be gifts. I didn't give your brother anything,' Kirsten lamented.

'You gave Prince Shahir a son,' an older woman piped up in astonishment. 'A son in the first year of marriage. He has been blessed enough.'

Kirsten gazed in shock at the delicately worked gold crown that emerged from the first box. It was light, and not over-large, but it was definitely a crown and not a tiara. Jahan lifted it with reverence and placed it on Kirsten's head. 'This has not been used since Shahir's mother, Bisma, died. You are honoured, for only our father, the King, could have offered it to you.'

There was an emerald necklace that flashed green fire, and it had been matched to drop earrings and a bracelet of fantastic design. Kirsten had never seen such fabulous jewellery, or dreamt that she might own it.

'The emerald set was made especially for you. The goldsmith and the designer worked day and night to finish them in time,' Jahan confided. 'You must be so happy that you have my brother's love.'

Kirsten veiled her gaze. 'Yes…'

'My mother was a second wife and less fortunate.' The other woman sighed. 'Shahir's mother was the King's first wife. She died of a seizure when Shahir was born and my father almost went mad with grief. He was urged by the people to marry again and have more sons. I was born, then my sister, and then Raza. My father could not love my mother as he felt she deserved and she was unhappy. In the end they divorced.'

'That's very sad,' Kirsten remarked, with a hollow feeling of threat in her tummy. She was trying not to wonder if some day Shahir would also decide that he was making her unhappy.

Jahan turned aside to speak to someone, and then turned back to Kirsten. 'Faria says it is time for us to go to the audience hall.'

Faria says. That was all Kirsten heard. Her green eyes lodged on the piquant face of the young woman. She was gorgeous, if a little sullen in expression. She had eyes that were the alluring shape of almonds, honey skin and a wealth of tumbling black curls. Kirsten felt huge and clumsy next to her, for the other woman was much smaller and yet surprisingly curvaceous in shape.

'You've gone white…don't be nervous,' Jahan whispered gently.

For goodness' sake, how common was that name? Faria? What reason did she have to believe that the Faria whom Shahir loved belonged to the privileged circle of those invited to attend the royal wedding? Faria might well live in another country, thousands and thousands of miles away, Kirsten told herself in urgent consolation.

The crown, she discovered, was heavier than it had initially seemed. She had to keep her back straight as an arrow and hold her head high to prevent it from slipping.

The audience hall was thronged with people. She exchanged a warm smile with her brother. Only when the crowds parted did she see Shahir. His brilliant dark eyes were sombre, his lean, bronzed features stunningly handsome below the crown he wore as if to the manner born. In his scarlet and black military uniform, with a sword hanging by his side, he was magnificent. As she drew level he reached for her hand, and the words of the marriage service were spoken in Arabic and then in English.

Shahir slid a gold ring that bore a crest on to the forefinger of her right hand. 'Now it is time for you to meet my father.'

King Hafiz received them in the privacy of an anteroom. He was a tall, sparely built bearded man, with astute dark eyes and a rather gloomy aspect. He did not speak English and Shahir acted as an interpreter. He bestowed his blessing on his son and daughter-in-law as both father and ruler. He raised Kirsten up from her deep curtsey and kissed her solemnly on either cheek, and told her through Shahir that she was so beautiful his son would only have had to look at her once to love her and see her smile to know that she had a true heart. He also came very near to smiling when he forecast that Tazeem would be the joy of his old age.

The festivities moved to a chamber where twin thrones

on a raised dais awaited the bride and groom. Jasmine blossoms were scattered round her feet and Kirsten was given a drink composed of honey and rose water. Traditional folk dances were performed. Poems were read. A lute player sang plaintive songs.

'Now, before we eat, you may change into something more appropriate…' Shahir informed her.

'Do I get to take off the crown?'

Vibrant amusement lit his eyes. 'Yes.'

'I know it's an honour to wear one, but it's hurting my neck.'

In a room down the corridor she was helped out of her ceremonial robe and shoes. She was astonished when a glorious white wedding dress was brought to her. The gown was a neat fit at breast and waist, accentuating her slender figure. A simple circlet of pearls was set on her head.

From the instant she reappeared and began moving down the room towards him Shahir's smouldering dark golden eyes were welded to her. A heady pink lit her cheeks and her mouth ran dry.

'You look amazing…you look as I dreamt you would look,' he confessed in an appreciative aside.

The wedding banquet was served, but she had no appetite for food. After the meal she was formally introduced to courtiers and officials. She saw Faria with a man who appeared to be her husband, and it looked very much as though the couple were having a fight. At least Faria had a tight mouth and seemed to be talking through gritted teeth while her companion seemed to be trying to placate her.

'That couple over there…who are they?' Kirsten finally asked Shahir.

His bold, classic profile tensed. 'My foster-sister and her husband.'

'What do you mean...*foster*-sister?'

'For several months her mother was my nurse after my own mother died in childbirth. In our society that relationship is viewed as the same as one formed by blood.'

Feeling as if she had hit the bullseye, Kirsten fixed her attention elsewhere. Her throat ached, for his tension and his every word had confirmed her suspicions. The exotic brunette *was* Faria, the woman he loved and could not have. Another man's wife and his foster-sister. She felt gutted, and her eyes were stinging like mad.

Raza strolled up and bent his dark head towards them. 'Have you been watching Faria? Do you remember how she always seemed to be all sweetness and light? What a shrew she's turned out to be!' he remarked with an exaggerated shudder. 'Poor Najim. He's an easygoing chap, and very clever, but he made a bad choice there. Watching Faria make a fool of him in public is enough to keep me single for ever!'

Kirsten's dulled eyes took on a sparkle of renewed animation. There was nothing appealing about a shrew, was there? She did not dare to look at Shahir lest she reveal her less than charitable feelings. Instead she gave Raza a big sunny smile.

'May I dance with the most beautiful bride ever to have entered this family?' Raza asked her winningly, down on one knee, hand clasped to his heart in melodramatic fashion.

As Kirsten laughed in appreciation of his sense of humour, Shahir rose upright in one powerful movement. 'Perhaps...after she has danced with me.'

His dark golden gaze shimmered over her flawless face and he extended a lean brown hand to lead her on to the floor. Suddenly she was very conscious of his raw masculinity and she lowered her eyes.

'I know what is on your mind,' Shahir murmured quietly. 'We will discuss it—but not here. We'll be leaving soon.'

Kirsten did not know how to dance in a formal way. She tripped over his feet and tried to head off in the wrong direction. The experience was sheer purgatory for her. Worse still, she was tormented by the conviction that he must have seen her staring at Faria. Had her interest been that obvious to him? Could he know what she had been thinking? The jealousy? The hatred? The evil thoughts? She really didn't want Shahir to have an accurate take on what went on in her mind

'You are a possessive husband,' Raza told his elder brother with lively amusement as the bridal couple left the floor. 'But on your wedding day I will forgive you.'

Rose petals and rice were scattered in front of Shahir and Kirsten as they walked out of the palace and got into a white limo adorned with streamers and flags.

'Now for the embarrassing stuff,' Shahir groaned, flashing her a rueful smile that made her heart jump inside her. 'Wave to the crowds as we pass.'

'Where are we going?'

'We're flying to my grandfather's palace at Zurak. Tazeem will join us tomorrow. But I do not wish to wait until we reach Zurak to say what I need to say to you.'

Kirsten stiffened and stole an apprehensive glance at him.

It was not a conversation Shahir wanted to have, but he knew he could not avoid the subject, for silence would encourage division. He breathed in deep. 'A long time ago I told you that I loved another woman.'

Kirsten shrugged both shoulders with overstated nonchalance while still waving and angling a fixed smile out at the crowds of spectators waiting for the royal motorcade to pass by. She behaved as though the issue of his loving another woman was of as much interest to her as watching paint dry. 'So?'

'As you now appear to be aware, I was referring to my foster-sister, Faria.'

Her wooden pretence of composure cracked and her pale head swivelled, green eyes flashing defensively. 'Am I that obvious?'

His dense black lashes screened his gaze. 'No. I am attuned to your mood now.'

The royal couple waved, and the silence stretched like an elastic band being yanked to breaking point.

'Don't keep me in suspense,' Kirsten breathed between clenched teeth.

'I do not find it easy to talk about feelings,' Shahir confessed in a driven undertone. 'But I do know that I should never have told you that I loved Faria.'

'Well...how were you to know that you were going to end up married to a woman with a memory like an elephant's?' Kirsten muttered waspishly, and it was awful because she could feel the tears gathering up behind her eyes like a dam ready to break.

'That is not the reason why I should not have made that statement. Since that day I have come to appreciate that I was mistaken about what I believed I felt,' Shahir disclosed tautly, his accent fracturing his words. 'I am not in love with her. I have never been in love with her. It was...I now see...no more than a foolish fancy.'

'Really?' Kirsten prompted chokily, thinking that he really had to think she was the stupidest woman in Dhemen to be telling her such a story on their wedding day.

Yet she understood what he was doing. When he had admitted that he loved Faria he had never dreamt that Kirsten would one day become his wife. Naturally he now wished he had kept quiet, and was keen to cover his tracks. Some dark secrets were better left buried. And how could she blame him for trying to hoodwink her? Recognising how jealous and insecure his bride was feeling, he was attempting to defuse the situation in the only way he could. He had told her a little white lie, the way well-meaning people lied to children sooner than reveal the cruel truth.

'You need never think of the matter again,' Shahir asserted with conviction.

'I won't.' At least not around him, she thought tragically.

A helicopter ferried them to the palace at Zurak. She gazed in wonder at the picturesque stone building. Surrounded on all sides by desert, the palace sat in the middle of a lush oasis of trees and greenery like a mirage.

'When my ancestors were nomads they stayed here in the heat of summer. My grandfather met my grandmother when she drew water from the well for him. It was love at first sight for them both. His father asked her father for her hand in marriage and that was that.' Shahir laughed and linked his fingers firmly with hers. 'Life was very much simpler in those days.'

'As long as you didn't have to draw the water from the well,' Kirsten could not resist pointing out.

'In all the great poems of the East men are portrayed as the more romantic sex,' Shahir informed her without skipping a beat. 'From the first moment I saw you, you were never out of my mind.'

That was lust, not love, she almost told him morosely. Did he think she had forgotten that every time he had touched her he had regretted it? Didn't he realise she still remembered that he had proposed marriage out of guilt at having taken her virginity? But their lives had moved on and they were married now. Furthermore, he was clever and he was practical. He wanted their marriage to be a success and naturally he was trying to make her feel good. Romance and compliments were part of the show, she reasoned.

She asked herself if that really mattered. Although he did not love her, she loved him, and she too wanted their relationship to work.

A fountain was playing in the centre of the tiled entrance hall. It was deserted. He pulled her gently round to face him and kissed her slow and deep, until she was dizzy with longing. She discovered that she no longer wanted to think about the fact that he was laying sensible foundations for a successful royal marriage.

Hand in hand, they walked up a wide marble staircase. Their footsteps echoed in the hot still air and the silence was magical after the noise and bustle of their wedding celebrations.

He thrust wide the door of a room at the end of the long gallery, and swept her up into his arms to carry her over the threshold. 'You look amazing in that dress...like you belong in a fairytale.'

He kicked shut the door in his wake and strolled almost indolently across the huge room to deposit her on a big four-poster bed. Silk and lace frothed round her in a highly feminine tangle of fabric.

'Oh, my goodness,' she gasped, tipping her head back to survey the map of the heavens painted on the vaulted ceiling far above.

'A bed with a view.' In the act of unbuttoning his military jacket, Shahir came down on the bed on one knee to claim her lush pink lips again, with a hunger that jolted her right down to her toes. 'But it will be morning before you have the time to admire it.'

'Is that a promise?' she asked breathlessly.

He unclasped the sword and set it aside with care before removing his jacket. 'Come here…'

Entrapped by the scorching gold of his scrutiny, she slid off the bed and approached him. He lifted the pearl circlet from her hair, gently turned her round and unzipped her gown. The dress tumbled round her knees and he lifted her free of the folds, hauling her back into the hard muscular heat of his masculine frame. The fine silk shift pulled taut over the pouting fullness of her unbound breasts and clung to skin that felt smooth and sensuous.

'You're so perfect, Your Serene Highness…' He sighed, his expert hands roaming over the pert mounds, massaging the rosy crowns into a swollen sensitivity that drew a breathless moan from her parted lips. Her head angled back, her silvery blonde hair falling like a sheet of polished silk across his shoulder. His mouth blazed a roving trail from her delicate jawbone to the pulse-point below her ear that made her jerk in response.

'Your Serene Highness…?' Kirsten echoed weakly, incomprehension gripping her at his form of address.

'My princess…my beautiful princess.' Shahir bent her forward to undo the tiny fasteners on the shift. 'The title comes courtesy of my father.'

The shift was being peeled down over the womanly curve of her hips and she could hardly breathe for anticipation, never mind carry on a sensible conversation. The pulse of desire throbbed an insistent beat between her thighs and her face was hot. 'I w-wasn't expecting it,' she stammered, shocked at the strength of what she was feeling.

'You deserve it—and more.' His rich drawl shimmied down her taut spine. 'You have gone through so much since I came into your life, *aziz*.'

'It wasn't all bad,' she confided unevenly.

'None of it should have been,' Shahir intoned, shedding his shirt.

Kirsten could not concentrate. Drawing her down on to the bed, he was caressing her lush little breasts with uninhibited masculine appreciation and skill. Her breath rasped back and forth in her throat as she struggled to stay in control. He lowered his proud dark head over the tormentingly tender tips that adorned the small ripe mounds and circled the stiff straining buds with the tip of his tongue. The onslaught of sensation was too much for her: her hips rose and she whimpered his name.

'Tonight…everything must be for your pleasure.' He straightened in one lithe movement and removed the remainder of his clothes.

Liquid heat danced over the delicate flesh at the heart of her. Even though she was taut with self-consciousness, and flushed with the shyness that even desire could not drive out, she couldn't drag her eyes from him.

'Why?' she whispered.

'The first time the pleasure was all mine.'

He had a stunning dark male beauty that mesmerised her. When she looked at him her heart pounded and she got butterflies in her tummy. His features were hard, sculpted and strong, brought to vibrant life by the dazzling dangerous gold of his eyes. He had the superb physique of an athlete. Lean muscle rippled below his bronzed skin, ebony curls delineating his powerful chest while a silky furrow of dark hair ran down in an intriguing line over his hard flat stomach. The bold thrust of his arousal ensnared her attention and filled her with sinful heat.

She was weak with longing when he came back to her, tasting her reddened mouth with hungry, marauding fervour. He worked his skilful passage down over her twisting, turning body, leaving a trail of fire wherever he lingered and parting her slender thighs. What he did next shocked her senseless, but before she could protest a wicked flood of unbearable sensation seized her and suddenly she had all the self-will of a remote controlled toy. Nothing could have prepared her for the sensual intensity of an experience that threatened to drive her out of her mind with an enjoyment so strong it came close to pain.

'Now...' Shahir framed with ragged force, pulling her beneath him when she could no longer stand the fierce need he had induced in her weak and unresisting body. With sure hands he tipped her up and plunged into the damp heated core of her with a harsh groan of wondering pleasure. 'It has never, ever been like this for me before...'

The raw passion of his possession sent such a shock wave of delight pulsing through her that she reached an instantaneous peak of ecstasy. The sweet violence of release gripped her in quivering spasms of joy until she was heavy and limp with satiation.

'Oh, Shahir...' she mumbled shakily.

In response he withdrew from her and turned her over, rearranging her on her knees.

'Shahir...?' she gasped in disconcertion.

He sank into her again, hard and fast, and she heard herself cry out with the intolerable pleasure of his entrance into her newly tender flesh. She had no thought after that. In fact wild excitement knocked every single thought out of her head. She abandoned herself to delight and more delight. Once more he drove her to the heights of an explosive climax, and with a cry of rapture she surrendered to the voluptuous waves of sweet pleasure that engulfed her.

When she recovered from that incredibly intense bout of passion Shahir was cradling her close. He had both arms wrapped round her while he scanned her delicate features with slumberous dark golden eyes full of appreciation. 'I will never let you out of my sight again, *aziz*. What a blessing it is that we found each other.'

Blissfully contented, and awash with love and security as Kirsten felt at that moment, she had, however, been disconcerted by one aspect of their lovemaking. She rested her cheek against a smooth brown muscular shoulder and murmured, 'You took precautions...'

'Of course...I won't run the risk of getting you pregnant again.'

Astonishment opened her green eyes to their fullest extent. 'But don't you want more children? I thought it sort of went with the territory,' she confided.

'Tazeem will have to be enough. Never again will I put you through birth...I could not do that to you,' Shahir admitted, a shudder of recollection rippling through the long lean body entwined with her softer curves. 'I found it very difficult to stand by while you were going through all that.'

A smile crept over Kirsten's full mouth. She snuggled closer to him. For weeks on end she had tormented herself with the belief that Shahir valued her mainly for her capacity to give him children. But he had just shown her how wrong she had been in that assumption. 'Is that because of what happened to your mother?' she whispered softly. 'Jahan mentioned how she had died.'

'It is true that my father has often spoken of that day

to me. Why not? It was the worst day of his life. But I wouldn't have discussed that tragedy while you were carrying our child,' Shahir countered. 'It would have disturbed you.'

He had been really worried about her, and yet he had kept his fears to himself rather than take the risk of frightening her with the story of his mother's sad demise. She was touched by his admission, and not for worlds would she have confided that she was just finding out that she had to be the most contrary woman alive on the planet. No sooner had Shahir assured her that Tazeem was to be their one and only child than she had decided that she wanted at least two more children. Once she'd realised that he valued her health more than her ability to have babies, her misgivings and sensitivity on that score had been vanquished for ever.

Shahir rolled her over and gazed down at her, inky black lashes low and sexy over striking dark golden eyes 'This is our wedding night...the talk is too serious.'

'But you're always serious.'

'Over the next few weeks you will learn that I have another side to my nature.'

'Weeks? How long have I got you for?' The instant that revealing question leapt off her tongue she wanted to cringe.

A wickedly attractive smile slashed his darkly handsome features. 'You have got me for at least six weeks...'

The pretence of cool could not contain her delight and she gasped, 'Six weeks? Honestly?'

'Honestly...and I intend for us to make full use of every priceless moment.' Matching words to action, Shahir captured her mouth with hungry urgency and let his tongue delve deep in an exploratory foray.

Tiny little darts of flame licked low in her pelvis. The

tender crests of her breasts tingled. Already she wanted to feel his hands on her again. Embarrassed though she was by her susceptibility, she couldn't resist him.

Reaching up to him in a helplessly encouraging movement, she let her fingers spear through the tousled depths of his black hair.

Shahir lifted his head again, his dark eyes reflective. 'You see, it will take every day of those weeks for you to learn royal etiquette and the history of our family...'

Kirsten blinked. 'I suppose...'

'And perhaps a little more Arabic.'

She nodded, seeing the solid sense of that as well.

Looking pensive, Shahir continued to study her. 'As my wife you should get to know the desert. The ability to ride a horse would be an advantage...and of course I could teach you to dance...'

Kirsten turned brick-red at that low reminder. 'It all sounds very educational.'

He unleashed his vibrant smile again. 'And the education will continue in private as well, while you teach me what you like,' he suggested huskily, letting a caressing hand curve to the swell of her hip as he brought her closer. 'And I teach you what I like...'

'But I might not have the energy to learn anything after all those lessons in etiquette, history and dancing.' Kirsten let her fingertips forge a provocative feminine trail down his taut flat stomach.

Shahir could not conceal his surprise or his instant fascination at that first show of boldness on her part. 'We'll make the time, *aziz*, ' he breathed unsteadily, hauling her to him with unsubtle force. 'Even if we have to stay here for ever!'

CHAPTER TEN

THE music Kirsten's nimble fingers coaxed from the piano keyboard in a rich flood of virtuoso notes flowed round the room and out into the corridor where the staff stood listening. The difficult technical passages of a Rachmaninoff prelude gave way to the fast upbeat rhythm of several Gershwin pieces, and finally to a dreamy waltz that soothed in the heat of midday when there was not a hint of a breeze in the air.

'If you hadn't married Shahir and become a besotted wife and mother, you might have become a great classical pianist,' her brother Daniel mused, reclining back in his seat in a lazy sprawl and sipping at a chilled lemon drink.

Kirsten laughed at the idea. Glazed doors had been folded back so that the room was open to the beautiful shaded courtyard beyond. Leaving the piano, she stepped over Squeak, who was snoozing in front of a whirling fan. She strolled out to sit down casually on a low wall beside Tazeem's pram. 'I'm not that good a player.'

'Oh, yes, you are. But you would have had to struggle to make a name for yourself in the music world, and you might never have got a lucky break. Instead you became a royal princess, with several palaces, legions of staff and a magnificent grand piano,' the young blond man quipped, watching her scoop his nephew out of the pram with loving maternal hands and proceed to cuddle him. 'There's no contest.'

'It's not all about what I've gained in material terms...I'm just happy,' Kirsten proclaimed a tad defensively as she dropped a kiss down on Tazeem's satin-smooth cheek.

'And you should be. Shahir spoils you rotten, I've got an open ticket to fly out here any weekend I want to see you—'

'Hasn't that been marvellous?' his sister interrupted with enthusiasm. 'We didn't have much time together at the wedding. But since then we've got to know each other again.'

'I must admit that it's no sacrifice to leave my student accommodation and enjoy three-course meals, a choice of swimming pools and servants on tap,' Daniel confided with engaging honesty. 'You are living an extraordinary life here.'

'Yes…' Kirsten gave him a dizzy smile.

'You wear diamonds one day, sapphires the next, and dazzling designer outfits you change every few hours. In fact you're better turned out than any Stepford Wife.'

Kirsten reddened and focused surprised eyes on him. 'I make an effort to look good. Is that a crime?'

Her sibling winced, looked as though he was about to speak, then apparently thought better of the idea and fell silent.

'What's wrong?' Kirsten prompted

'Well, I wasn't planning to comment, and maybe I should mind my own business…but sometimes it seems like you're trying so hard to be perfect at everything that you're stressing yourself out.'

It was such an astute comment that she paled and screened her eyes. 'Did Shahir say something to you?'

'Of course not.' Daniel fielded an instant rebuttal. 'Shahir would never dream of talking about you behind your back. Look, forget what I said. I don't know what I'm talking about.'

An hour later, he was on his way to the airport and a return flight to London. It had been his third visit in two months, and Kirsten had thoroughly enjoyed the time they had spent together. At the same time, however, Shahir's relatives had welcomed her warmly into *their* lives, and she had become particularly close to his sister, Jahan.

Shahir and Kirsten spent most weekends at Zurak, but weekdays were generally spent at the Ahmet, where they had the privacy of their own palace.

It was hard for her to believe that she had been living in Dhemen for two months on what felt like an extended honeymoon.

Those first few weeks of togetherness with Shahir at Zurak had been sheer, unadulterated bliss. The passion between them had burned hotter than hot, turning day into night and night into day. The wildness of the pleasure they had found in each other still shocked her. It was as though their desire was never fully assuaged. Shahir walked into a room and she wanted him. Sitting through a meal, getting through a polite conversation with visitors could be a private torment. Without the slightest encouragement she would find herself recalling the aromatic scent of his skin, the taste of him and the hard heat of his urgent body against hers, and occasionally it mortified her to be at the mercy of a hunger she could not control.

No onlooker would ever have guessed that Shahir was not in love with his wife, for he managed to act as though Kirsten was the centre of his world. He had shared so much more with her than a bed, she acknowledged, wanting to give honour where it was due. He had taken her into the desert to see the sun go down in crimson splendour, and there he had introduced her to the exquisite and unforgettable love poetry of Kahlil Gibran. He had also tried commendably hard not to laugh when she ran screaming from a lizard she had mistaken for a snake.

He rarely came home without a gift for her or Tazeem. It might be a single flower, a book, a toy for their son or an extravagant jewel, but he gave with immense generosity. He had told her about the harsh routine of the military school he had attended, and the rather disconcerting freedom that had been his when he'd later studied business at Harvard. She had begun to understand the forces and influences that had forged his reserve.

On a visit to a Beduoin encampment she had watched him take part in a sword dance and a camel race, and she had secretly savoured that glimpse of the wild side of his volatile temperament which he kept under such fierce control. They had spent the night in a tent bedecked with ancient rugs, and he had spread her out on the floor and made passionate love to her until dawn, masking her every moan with his mouth so that they would not be heard. In the morning she had watched him fly his peregrine falcon high and free, and he had told her that that was how she made him feel in bed.

She was madly in love with him, but she tried not to think too much about that. Such reflections tended to make her dwell on the fact that he was not in love with her. She tried not to remember that dreadfully stilted exchange on their wedding day, when he had tried to lay her fears about Faria to rest. She was willing to believe that he had never spoken a word of forbidden love to his gorgeous foster-sister. And she thought it was equally likely that Faria had no idea of how Shahir felt about her. But Kirsten was constantly aware that the man she loved had given his heart to another woman, and no matter how happy she was that knowledge was like a raw place on her soul that would not heal.

Somehow her brother had sensed that kernel of insecurity buried deep down inside her. She *did* strive to be the perfect wife. She took great care of her appearance and, although her cheeks warmed at this reflection, she knew she had been a fast learner in the bedroom. As she had a husband who was currently suffering considerable ribbing from his family for flying back from London just to spend two hours with her before leaving again, she was fairly certain she was meeting the right targets in that area of their relationship. She was equally diligent with lessons in Arabic and etiquette, and already knew more about the history of Shahir's family than he did.

'Kirsten...?' Shahir appeared in the doorway.

Her green eyes lit up. She flew down the length of the grand reception room and flung herself at him. He caught her up in his arms, but instead of kissing her as he usually did he set her gently and carefully back from him. Lean strong face grave, he rested his hands on her slim shoulders and surveyed her with strained dark golden eyes.

'What's wrong?' she pressed, a sliver of unease fingering down her spine.

'Pamela Anstruther is here in person to plead her case with you. Do you wish to see her?'

'Pamela...*Lady Pamela*?' Her smooth brow divided. 'Plead her case? What are you talking about?'

Shahir straightened to his full commanding height. 'I was planning to tell you tonight that the allegation of theft that was laid against you at Strathcraig has finally been disproved.'

Her lashes fluttered wide, her astonishment palpable. 'Has it?'

'Unfortunately neither of the two women who accused

you had anything to gain from admitting the truth. Both had committed a criminal offence. That is why it has taken such a long time to sort out this matter,' Shahir explained heavily.

'But you kept on trying?' Kirsten was impressed by the commitment he had brought to the challenge of refuting the charges made against her.

'Yes, of course I did. Unfortunately the continual round of interviews and questions carried out by my personal staff did not appear to be bearing fruit.'

'But they were still working on it all the same. I was afraid to ask you what was happening in case you'd given up,' Kirsten confided in a rush.

His clear eyes met hers levelly. 'I would not have done that.'

'How has the theft charge been disproved?'

'I understand that the assistant housekeeper, Morag Stevens, finally confessed yesterday that she had lied. She accepted a financial bribe from Pamela Anstruther to plant the pendant in your locker and act as a false witness against you.'

Kirsten could not hide her disgust. 'So why did Morag confess after all this time?'

'Pamela was afraid that Morag would crack under the pressure of the questions being asked. In an attempt to frighten Morag into continuing to keep quiet Pamela made the mistake of threatening her. Morag panicked and admitted everything she had done to the housekeeper.'

'So my name has been cleared?' Kirsten nodded to herself with satisfaction even as she frowned in puzzlement. 'But I don't understand why Lady Pamela would come all the way to Dhemen to see me.'

Beneath his bronzed complexion, Shahir seemed very pale. 'The woman is facing prosecution. I have already interviewed her. Our meeting was brief. I see no reason why she should escape punishment. Perhaps she hopes to awaken your pity. Remember that she had none for you.'

More troubled by his bleak attitude than by Pamela's arrival at the Ahmet Palace, Kirsten shook her head as though to clear it. 'To be honest, I'm in shock at all this.'

'You don't have to see her. Such a person is beneath your notice.'

'I would like to hear what she has to say for herself.' Kirsten's chin came up at a determined angle. 'But I really don't want her to enter our home.'

'It will not be necessary for her to do so.'

Shahir escorted her to a large building situated nearest the entrance to the Ahmet complex. It housed the offices of the senior courtiers, the administrative block, and the reception rooms used for formal public occasions. When he would have accompanied her into a small audience hall, she informed him that she would prefer to see Pamela alone.

'As you wish...then I will leave you.'

His formality offended her. She was on a high: her name had been cleared, her reputation cleansed, her innocence of theft proven. But Shahir, infuriatingly, was behaving as though someone had died.

As Kirsten passed by a tall gilded mirror, she realised what a staggering change Lady Pamela would now see in her. Her eloquent mouth quirked. Pearls glistened in her ears and round her throat. Her turquoise and pink wrap top, matching tiered skirt and fine pink leather pumps were the very latest in designer style.

Two of the élite palace guards were stationed in the hall where Pamela was waiting. Kirsten gave them a nod of dismissal. The brunette looked worn and tired, and her dress was badly creased.

'Your Serene Highness…' Pamela performed a low and very creditable curtsey without hesitation. 'Thank you for seeing me.'

'I just want to know why you did it.'

Pamela Anstruther fixed incredulous china-blue eyes on her. 'Because Prince Shahir was in love with you, of course…why else?'

Kirsten was paralysed to the spot by that retort. 'I beg your pardon?'

Pamela's mouth took on a resentful curve. 'I was mad for him too. I hated you for getting in the way.'

'You were jealous?'

'I saw the Prince with you twice—in the limo the day he offered you a lift, and the day I invited him for tea. The way he looked at you was really quite nauseating,' the brunette contended with a bitter laugh. 'He couldn't hide it. You were just a farm girl, but I could practically hear the wedding bells ringing. It was like you had cast a spell on him—and yet you were so naive that you didn't even *see* the power you had.'

'If you disliked me so much why did you ask me to help you with the party preparations?'

Pamela heaved a weary sigh. 'Right from the start I planned to have you accused of stealing. I wanted you out of the castle and away from him. But I didn't want to harm you personally—'

'Really?' Kirsten cut in very dryly.

'Really,' Pamela insisted. 'It was simply a case of needs must. I had no hope of getting anywhere with the Prince while you were around.'

'So you decided to frame me for theft? You ensured that I found that brooch while Shahir was in the next room and that was your first step towards setting me up to be accused of stealing, wasn't it?'

'I'm not denying what I did. I bribed silly little Morag to lie and stick the pendant in your locker. But I had no luck, did I? You're years younger than I am, and perfectly beautiful. Your Prince was obsessed with you and he married you all the same. And Morag got cold feet and dropped us both in it.' Pamela Anstruther settled defiant blue eyes on Kirsten. 'I'm ruined anyway. I'll have to sell up and leave the glen. I can't live there now that everyone knows what I did to you. I'm getting the cold shoulder everywhere.'

'That's not my fault.'

'No, but do I really deserve to be dragged into court and prosecuted into the bargain? After all, it's pretty obvious that Prince Shahir would have married you even if you had murdered someone!' Pamela pointed out sourly. 'I'm sorry I ever tangled with the pair of you. I'm sorry that I had you accused of something you didn't do and that you lost your job. But I do feel the need to point out that it doesn't seem to have harmed your social prospects much.'

Kirsten treated the other woman to a cool appraisal, and it took the self-discipline that Shahir had patiently taught her to prevent her from succumbing to an inappropriate desire to laugh. 'I believe I've heard enough. Go back to the UK. I'll think over what you've said, but I'm not making any promises.'

Without another word, her mind buzzing with feverish thoughts, Kirsten left the audience chamber and walked briskly back to the huge rambling palace that had been designated as her home and Shahir's. A palace within a palace, it rejoiced in its own high walls and the seclusion and the wonderful steam room she had enjoyed on her wedding day.

All Kirsten could really think about was Pamela's unswerving conviction that Shahir loved his wife. She was also starting to appreciate why Shahir had been under so much strain when he had last spoken to her: he would be devastated by the realisation that he had misjudged her. He set himself such impossibly high standards and tore himself up over every error. Hadn't she already learned that he was his own fiercest critic?

She heard her royal husband's voice before she saw him. Wondering who he was talking to, she tiptoed over to the door of his study and peered in.

'I blew it,' Shahir was saying morosely. 'I always blow it with her. I say the wrong thing…I do the wrong thing. How am I supposed to tell her that I didn't really care if she was a thief any more? That doesn't sound right, does it? It sounds crazy, but that's how it was. I had stopped thinking about it.'

His confessor loosed a sympathetic sigh as his floppy ears were stroked. Short stubby tail wagging gently, the little dog curled up at Shahir's feet and lay down to sleep.

'You should be talking to me, not Squeak,' Kirsten declared.

Shahir leapt upright in surprise and swung round in a fluid arc. A dark line of colour scored his proud, angular cheekbones. 'I didn't expect you to return this quickly.'

'Pamela is so self-obsessed she's not good company,' Kirsten quipped, moving in a restive prowl round the room, because she was so nervous that she could not stay still. 'I've decided that I don't want charges pressed against her or Morag. Presumably Morag Stevens has been sacked?'

'Of course.'

'Let that be enough, then. I just want the whole thing dropped and forgotten about now.'

'But you were deliberately singled out to suffer Pamela

Anstruther's malicious attacks on your reputation. What those women did was criminal.'

'I was the victim, but you were the cause. No, believe me, I'm not blaming you for being so fanciable that Pamela Anstruther was willing to break the law to discredit me in your eyes.' Reluctant amusement shone in Kirsten's gaze as Shahir slung her a disconcerted look. 'But what she did does seem to have been girlie warfare of the nastiest kind—and that's what it was all about. Of course I expect she was after your money as well as—'

'I imagine so,' Shahir slotted in, before she could elaborate on what else he might have to offer in the fanciable department. 'You are choosing to take a strangely light-hearted view of this affair.'

'Affair? Did you ever…with Pamela, I mean?' Kirsten suddenly prompted in horror, mentally crossing her fingers and praying that he had not.

Shahir spread two lean brown hands wide, his shock and embarrassment at finding himself the target of so intimate a question patent. 'Of course not.'

'But maybe you were just a little tempted by her before I came along?'

'Her manner was so encouraging that I may have considered the possibility once or twice.' His even white teeth were visibly gritted as he forced out that admission. 'But I maintained a formal distance with her and ultimately her boldness offended me.'

'Thank you for telling me that,' Kirsten murmured gently. 'I can now see how Pamela might have thought she had a chance with you and that I spoilt it.'

'That would be nonsense, and it should not influence your opinion of what she did to you.'

'You're not a woman, Shahir. You don't understand.'

But he was *so* honest. Kirsten marvelled at how honest

he was. She wanted to apologise for getting so personal, but she was impressed that he would tell the truth even when to do so affronted his fierce pride. Now she wondered how she had ever dared to doubt his word.

Lean strong face bleak, Shahir straightened his shoulders like a soldier facing up to a firing squad. 'You must allow me to offer you my profound regret for not having had faith in you when you were accused of stealing. I—'

'That's fine—it's OK. Pamela's clever, and that stunt she pulled with the brooch really did make me look very guilty.'

'Please let me say what I must,' Shahir incised.

Kirsten fell silent, frustration filling her—for she had wanted to discuss something that was much more important to her.

'I am ashamed that you came to me for help and I would not believe that you were telling me the truth. I did let you down,' he asserted, not quite levelly. 'That will live with me until the day I die.'

I know it will,' she muttered helplessly, wishing he didn't take everything quite so much to heart. 'But you are only human.'

Strained dark golden eyes sought and held hers. 'You left home without money or proper support. Any one of a number of appalling fates might have become yours. Throughout the seven months it took for me to find you I was haunted by fear for your wellbeing.'

Kirsten nodded thoughtfully. 'Even before you knew I was pregnant?'

'Yes…and that discovery made my betrayal of your trust all the more unforgivable,' he reasoned grittily.

Kirsten lifted her head high, green eyes full of resolve. 'I forgive you.'

Shahir frowned. 'But you cannot—'

'If I say I forgive you, I forgive you!'

'Yes, but—'

'Is *my* forgiveness *mine* to give or not?' Kirsten suddenly shot at him in exasperation.

Shahir paled and compressed his beautiful mouth into an austere line. 'Of course it is yours to give.'

'Then you're just going to have to live with being forgiven for thinking you were married to a thief.' Studying his darkly handsome features, Kirsten felt her heartbeat accelerate, and tried not to smile because he was being so very serious. 'We didn't know each other when Tazeem was conceived. That was the real problem. We had all that physical attraction going for us and complicating things, but we were still almost strangers.'

Shahir looked pensive. 'I had not thought of it from that angle. You are right. Trust takes time to build. But I had never known a hunger such as you awakened in me,' he confided, half under his breath. 'It was like a fire that burned out my common sense and control. I saw you and I was lost. I fought it and the fire kept on blazing up, destroying all my good intentions.'

'I didn't help you stick to your good intentions when I lied and said I wasn't a virgin. Don't keep on talking as if only one of us was in charge of events.'

A rueful laugh was wrenched from Shahir. 'I was not in charge at all. With hindsight I see that when Pamela suggested you were not as innocent as you seemed I wanted to believe it because it made you seem more within reach.'

Temper sparking, Kirsten exclaimed, 'What did that witch say about me?'

'Foolish insinuations which I know to be untrue—for you were pure until I took advantage of you,' Shahir stated soothingly.

Feeling that her being taken advantage of was not a direction she wanted their dialogue to travel in, Kirsten changed the subject to the one that had been on her mind from the minute she'd rushed to find him. 'On our wedding day you told me you didn't love Faria…'

His imperious dark brows rose in surprise. 'I don't.'

'But, you see, I didn't believe you. I assumed you were just saying that to cover up the truth and keep me happy.'

He viewed her with candid bewilderment. 'I would not have deceived you.'

Excitement was beginning to nip at Kirsten. He had been telling the truth when he'd said he no longer loved Faria!

Shahir grimaced. 'Perhaps I was not very convincing when I tried to explain about Faria, but I was most embarrassed. To reach my age and to realise that I had never been in love—'

'Never?' she whispered in wonderment.

'It wasn't until I met you that I realised that the emotions you inspired far surpassed anything I had ever felt for Faria. I then felt very foolish. I had mistaken a moment of admiration, a daydream, for the real thing.'

Kirsten reached hurriedly for his hands and tugged him closer, fingers curving into his and clinging like mad. 'So you were saying…?' she encouraged.

Anxious dark golden eyes gazed down into hers and his hands tightened in the hold of hers. 'I think I may have fixed on the dream of Faria, who was conveniently out of reach, as an excuse to avoid the threat of having to marry when I didn't want to.'

Kirsten shifted enticingly closer, freeing one hand to slide it up over a broad shoulder. 'It really doesn't matter. What does matter is that when you took me into the desert and read all that gorgeous love poetry to me you were being romantic.'

'What else?'

'Because you *felt* romantic—not because being romantic was what you thought of as a duty on your honeymoon.'

Shahir looked indisputably lost as he attempted to work out that statement.

'I've been so stupid... Of course, if you'd just *said*.' Kirsten gave his tie a little admonitory tug as she began to unknot it. 'Just said you loved me, then I would have known and I would have told you how I feel about you.'

Shahir trailed loose his tie and unbuttoned his collar with rare clumsiness. 'So I just say...I love you?' he breathed unevenly.

'And I say... Fancy that? I love you too. I've been in love with you ever since you swooped up on that dangerous motorbike and almost ran Squeak over.'

They stared at each other, absorbing their respective expressions. A joyful smile had illuminated her face and a glow of happiness had banished his gravity and tension.

'I think that must have been when it happened to me too. I never knew a happy moment after that until we were safely married,' Shahir confided. 'But how can you love me when I have made so many mistakes?'

'Stop arguing about it...you're loved,' Kirsten told him.

'I thought you were only marrying me because you were pregnant.'

'And I thought that was the only reason you asked me.'

'You could not have believed that the first time I proposed at the castle,' Shahir pointed out. 'At that stage it hadn't occurred to either of us that you might have conceived.'

'No, but I thought you were proposing out of guilt.'

He closed his arms round her and crushed her to him in a fierce embrace. 'There was some guilt, I admit,' he told her huskily. 'But much more love and desire was involved. Regrettably, I didn't understand my own heart that day—and the accusation of theft against you shocked me and divided us. Had that not occurred I would have realised within days that you were the woman I wanted to share the rest of my life with. Instead I let you down—'

'No…no…no. No more of that,' Kirsten scolded, resting an admonitory forefinger to his beautifully shaped mouth.

He pressed his lips to the centre of her palm and then lowered his head to savour her lush mouth with reverent appreciation. 'I love you so much it hurts,' he admitted gruffly. 'Never again do I want to relive those months of searching and fearing that I would never see you again.'

Her hands slid below his jacket and across his lean, muscular chest. With a ragged groan of response he devoured her mouth again. Kisses interspersed with passionate declarations of devotion followed, until matters became so heated that Shahir swept Kirsten off to the privacy of their bedroom…

Eighteen months later, Kirsten bustled round the spacious nursery at Strathcraig Castle until Tazeem finally and reluctantly dropped off to sleep. Her toddler's boundless reserves of energy never failed to amaze her, and he had enjoyed a very sociable day. Now, with his black lashes resting on his cheeks like silk fans, he looked like an angel. That idea made her grin, for he could be as naughty as any other child and she had to learn to be firm with him.

Earlier that day Shahir and Kirsten had thrown a huge Christmas party for the tenants, the staff and their neighbours, and a very good time had been had by all. King Hafiz, who had become a regular visitor at his son and daughter-in-law's Scottish castle, had laughed uproariously at the antics of the clowns hired to entertain the children. And even the latest additions to Shahir and Kirsten's family circle had managed to stay awake later than usual.

But now their infant son, Amir, and their daughter, Bisma, were slumbering in perfect peace in their adjoining cots. These twins had been a surprise package, for their arrival had not been planned.

In fact Kirsten had not even got round to tackling Shahir about his fear of her undergoing childbirth again before she had realised that she was already pregnant again. She had discovered that spontaneous passion in the steam room could have consequences—quite delightful consequences, she reflected, regarding her eight-week-old twins with fond maternal pride.

Amir and Bisma had been born without surgical intervention. Shahir had still looked rather faint once or twice during the proceedings, but had held up valiantly to the challenge.

Indeed, the past year and a half of married life had been blissfully happy for Kirsten. Secure in her husband's love and admiration, she made occasional appearances in support of various charitable enterprises in Dhemen, and she was now much too busy and much too content to worry about trying to be the perfect wife all the time.

Her brother Daniel had achieved his doctorate, and was currently employed on a conservation project in the

Arabian Gulf. He was able to visit his sister in Dhemen as often as he liked.

There had, however, been a less happy conclusion to Kirsten's attempt to mend fences with her father. Her letters had been returned unopened, and six months earlier Angus Ross had passed away suddenly after suffering a heart attack. Daniel and Kirsten had attended the funeral and paid their last respects with sadness, but also with acceptance that they had done what they could to re-establish contact with the older man. Perhaps it was for that reason that Kirsten had increasingly come to rely on and appreciate the love, kindness and support she had found within Shahir's family.

'We have two nannies and a host of other helpful staff,' Shahir remarked from the threshold of the room, Squeak trotting at his heels. 'But where do I still find you?'

'The same place I often find you at the end of the day. Has the King retired for the night?' Kirsten asked as she accompanied her tall, handsome husband along the passage to their bedroom.

'Yes, and I've booked the clowns for his birthday this summer. I haven't seen my father enjoy himself that much in years. I know who to thank for that too.' Shahir gave her a warmly appreciative smile. 'My royal parent has never liked traveling, but you have organised his suite here exactly as his rooms are at home and he seems very relaxed.'

'I'm glad.'

Curving a possessive arm round her slender back, Shahir slowly welded her soft, yielding curves to his lean, muscular frame and murmured huskily, 'I really love being married to you. '

'Do you?' A highly provocative and feminine smile tilted her mouth.

The answering glitter of his stunning dark golden eyes made her mouth run dry. 'I'm crazy about you.'

As Shahir splayed his fingers to the swell of her hip, to ease her into even closer contact, Kirsten stretched up her arms to link them round his neck. 'I love you too…so much.'

He bent his proud dark head and circled her lush pink lips with his own. She quivered in wild response. He kissed her breathless. He told her how happy she made him. He told her that without her and the children his life would have no meaning.

Kirsten listened starry-eyed while Squeak yawned, and yawned again. He had seen it all before, and he headed off to his cosy basket in the room next door and snuggled down to sleep.

HARLEQUIN Presents

The Arranged Brides

Settling a score—and winning a wife!

Don't miss favorite author Trish Morey's brand-new duet

PART ONE: STOLEN BY THE SHEIKH

Sapphire Clemenger is designing the wedding gown for Sheikh Khaled Al-Ateeq's chosen bride. Sapphy must accompany the prince to his exotic desert palace, and is forbidden to meet his future wife. She begins to wonder if this woman exists....

**Part two: The Mancini Marriage Bargain
Coming in March 2006**

www.eHarlequin.com

HPTAB0206

**She's sexy, successful
and pregnant!**

Share the surprises, emotions,
drama and suspense as our
parents-to-be come to terms
with the prospect of bringing a new life into the world.
All will discover that the business of making babies
brings with it the most special joy of all....

THE SICILIAN'S
DEFIANT MISTRESS

by Jane Porter

Tycoon Maximos Borsellino made a deal with Cass for
sex. Now that Cass wants more from him, he ends the
affair. Cass is heartbroken—worse, she
discovers she's pregnant....

On sale this February.

www.eHarlequin.com

HPEXP0206

HARLEQUIN *Presents*

GREEK TYCOONS

They're the men who have everything—except brides....

Wealth, power, charm—what else could a heart-stoppingly handsome tycoon need? In the GREEK TYCOONS miniseries you can meet gorgeous Greek multimillionaires who are in need of wives.

Don't miss out on BABY OF SHAME...

BABY OF SHAME
by Julia James

Rhianna has struggled through poverty and illness, dedicating herself to her son.

Now Alexis Petrakis has discovered that their shame-filled night created a beautiful baby he's determined to reclaim....

BABY OF SHAME on sale February 2006.

www.eHarlequin.com

HPGT0206